PETER'S COTTAGE

PETER'S COTTAGE
AN OLD STORY WITH SOME NEW TWISTS

D. V. HAINES

Copyright © 2021 D.V. Haines

The moral right of the author has been asserted.

Apart from any fair dealing for the purposes of research or private study, or criticism or review, as permitted under the Copyright, Designs and Patents Act 1988, this publication may only be reproduced, stored or transmitted, in any form or by any means, with the prior permission in writing of the publishers, or in the case of reprographic reproduction in accordance with the terms of licences issued by the Copyright Licensing Agency. Enquiries concerning reproduction outside those terms should be sent to the publishers.

This is a work of fiction. Names, characters, businesses, places, events and incidents are either the products of the author's imagination or used in a fictitious manner. Any resemblance to actual persons, living or dead, or actual events is purely coincidental.

Matador
9 Priory Business Park,
Wistow Road, Kibworth Beauchamp,
Leicestershire. LE8 0RX
Tel: 0116 279 2299
Email: books@troubador.co.uk
Web: www.troubador.co.uk/matador
Twitter: @matadorbooks

ISBN 978 1800464 681

British Library Cataloguing in Publication Data.
A catalogue record for this book is available from the British Library.

Printed and bound in the UK by TJ Books Limited, Padstow, Cornwall
Typeset in 11pt Adobe Garamond Pro by Troubador Publishing Ltd, Leicester, UK

Matador is an imprint of Troubador Publishing Ltd

If there were dreams to sell,
Merry and sad to tell,
And the crier rang the bell,
What would you buy?

A cottage lone and still,
With bowers nigh,
Shadowy, my woes to still
Until I die,
This would I buy.

**Thomas Beddoes,
1803-1849.**
(from **Dream-Pedlary**)

Contents

Chapter		Page
One	Clematis Montana	1
Two	Very Peculiar Behaviour	18
Three	Honey From The Meadow-Bees	31
Four	Another Part of the Heart	44
Five	Back to the Cottage	74
Six	Well Done	93
Seven	A Call from the Cottage	112

CHAPTER ONE

Clematis Montana

I

It was on a Thursday in the first week in June that Peter came out of the front door of his cottage.

He shut the door with lingering care. Also, he did quite a bit of lingering in walking down the path to the garden gate.

He had to duck his head slightly because of the Clematis Montana over-arching the gate. He opened the gate and then closed it behind him. The clematis was in bloom and showeringly white and heart-achingly beautiful, but this was a beauty with a reputation for too short a life. He sighed in giving it a quick glance.

He was carrying an adequate overnight-bag – a smart leather suitcase; and he was wearing an extremely well-cut suit. His collar and tie were crisply centred. Cuff-links? Yes, but discreetly visible.

Was he, perhaps, a chief accountant? He was not, but he looked like one – except that he was not wearing the bowler hat supposedly so typical of that species. His hat was a very fetching trilby, dark blue.

"Good morning, sir," said the village taxi-driver.

He was standing almost at attention in holding open the rear passenger door.

"Good morning, Percy," said Peter, serious but remaining good-humoured. "Do you think I shall need my umbrella?"

"Oh I very much doubt it. The next few days look like being lovely all times over."

"Even so," said Peter, profoundly hesitating, "an Englishman and his umbrella are seldom parted. That's a very old saying. It's not wise to ignore it. On the other hand, I do have my raincoat with me," which was folded over his other arm.

"I reckons that will be sufficient, sir. But you won't catch the train you say you want – not if you delays much longer."

Peter took off his hat to enter the taxi (his suitcase and the raincoat went in the boot).

For most of the drive to Woodley Norton – the nearest railway-town to the cottage – he stayed silent and as still as a rock. The only movement he slowly made was half-way through the drive when he turned his head. Not a happy turn of the head. It was for gazing through the tightly-shut window at the passing Oxfordshire scenery. He was gazing as if it were passing from his life for ever.

He actually shuddered when the taxi came to rest outside Woodley Norton's inoffensive railway-station. He was giving us every impression of a man on his way, if not to his execution, to a highly unpleasant appointment. Why was he apparently so unable to cope with it? After all, he was a man in obvious splendid health. Although exactly fifty, he had an enviable full head of fair hair and looked much younger (to the annoyance of others).

He put on the fetching trilby after getting out of the taxi, almost forgetting (in his state of gloom) to add a tip.

"Thank you, sir," said the taxi-driver, who, being a kindly man, had ushered Peter from the taxi as if helping a delicate invalid.

"What ever your doings are going to be on this day, sir," said this taxi-driver, "you is going to be lucky. I bet you anything. This is your lucky day."

Peter thanked him politely but without a smile. His mind

was now very much elsewhere. He bought his ticket for London (Paddington) without even noticing that the booking-hall was oddly devoid of all other people, except the clerk who seemed to be a total stranger. Similarly, in drifting out on the platform to await the train, Peter didn't notice that he seemed to be the only waiting passenger.

Woodley Norton was not a small railway-station. Normally, it would be at least briskly half-busy on a Thursday morning, but we all have to note one important matter. This whole adventure of Peter's was in the now historic times of British Rail. The last vestiges of its eccentricity had yet to be "privatised" by one Mr John Major. It should be no surprise to us that Peter's adventure included a steam-train.

Yes, steam. And with carriages to match.

It came into the station so promptly that Peter was startled and annoyed. One solitary porter had appeared on the platform. He blew harshly on his old-fashioned whistle. Peter had to yank open the nearest carriage-door and scramble aboard unaided. The porter (not a kindly man like the taxi-driver) slammed the door on Peter as if it were a cell-door in the Bastille.

Again, Peter didn't really notice that the entire train seemed as empty as the station.

The corridor was incredibly narrow. It lurched this way and that as the train, all too quickly for Peter, snorted up to speed.

He slid open the nearest possible door to a first-class compartment. Amazingly, there were six massively upholstered seats within – three aside and facing each other. Out of breath, Peter threw his suitcase up the rack above one of the seats, then his precautionary raincoat. He slumped down on the seat beneath. He was still wearing his trilby, his fetching trilby in dark blue. He closed his eyes for all of five seconds.

Being so preoccupied for reasons we have yet to discover, he had not been aware of someone else in the otherwise empty compartment.

A woman's voice quietly made itself heard. "You don't recognise me, do you? You've forgotten me."

II

She was sitting on the side opposite to Peter, but in the far corner by the picture-window. Her face was soft and faraway-looking, as if drawn in light pastel-chalk on terracotta paper.

His downcast mood instantly changed, although he opened his eyes and stood up trembling. He removed his hat and said: "Of course I haven't forgotten you!"

He said this so feelingly that he sounded curt, which he hadn't meant to be.

Moving to the seat opposite her and sitting down, he could only gaze at her for a few moments before saying: "There's not been a day when I've not thought of you. Not one single day."

"Nor I you," this woman said, nestling back a little. "Nor I you. Twenty-two years – nearly twenty-three."

"I've counted them," said Peter, a lot less curtly and now in a state of joyful wonderment.

Their rapport was instantaneous as if there had been no interval. Both began to laugh at each other, helplessly and gently.

"What I can't really understand now," she said, looking sweetly mystified, "is how it is you look so much the same. Hardly changed at all."

"That's nonsense, madam. I was twenty-eight when I saw you. I was often classified in those days as a mere youth. You're the one who hasn't changed."

"I'm forty five, so don't be silly," but she was very contented with the compliment.

And we can say it was reasonably justified. She looked charmingly and brightly healthy, and so slim and pocket-sized that Peter was already longing to protect her for the rest of his life. He actually found it difficult to believe she was real. The taxi-driver had been right, hadn't he? This was turning out to be Peter's lucky day. More than lucky, Peter was heart-thumpingly telling himself. No other woman had ever had this instant effect upon him. Even at forty-five, she was invitingly feminine in her refreshingly elegant summer-dress. And her hair (of course!) seemed to Peter as enticingly dark as when he saw her in their youthful past.

Even the cheekily stylish little hat was entrancing him. The only inconsistency he was faintly aware of was that she had no luggage for an obviously major journey. All she had with her was a typical handbag which (of course!) matched the gloves she was wearing.

Peter sat forward, tactfully and hopefully.

He managed to say (because his voice was a bit broken up and husky): "Ought we, perhaps, to introduce ourselves? Is this acceptable to you?"

"Highly acceptable," was her quick reply. "I can't stop myself from saying so. I can't be subtle about it."

For all of his fifty-years, Peter was in many ways naïve. He innocently said: "I've always supposed that women in love are far more subtle than men."

"You're wrong," he was swiftly told. "Only a woman playing at love can be subtle. Believe me, I know it. I've learnt it. A woman genuinely in love is far too scared to be subtle. Scared to death."

"I see what you mean," said Peter, not seeing at all. "Scared to death, you say?"

"To death, yes. As I am. Scared to death of losing sight of you yet again – and for ever. So tell me your name," she commanded, but with a softly endearing little laugh.

"My name is Peter," said Peter.

"Oh, that's a lovely name! I should have known you were called Peter. It means rock. No other name would suit you. But Peter what?"

"Peter Smith," he rather apologetically replied. "I hope that's all right? It's not exactly the most resounding of names, as I've often been told."

Again that softly endearing laugh.

"Smith eh? Not a surname which, if I had known it, would have made things easier to me to try tracking you down. But it's a wonderful name. Peter Smith. The names go so well together I could cry," and her voice did break slightly as if she might do so.

Hastily, Peter said: "Do please tell me. What is your name?"

She answered almost in a whisper. "Timothea."

It was now Peter's turn to be rendered ecstatic.

"Oh, what a lovely name! Timothea! I've never even heard of it before. But Timothea what?"

"Gudgeon."

Peter was equally delighted with this name and he said: "I don't think I've ever heard of that name either!"

"Look it up in a dictionary as soon as you can. It's the name for a small fish used as bait."

"Really? I've never been aware of that. I'm no fisherman. But I could have traced you quite easily, I'm sure, if I'd known you were a gudgeon."

Timothea took off her gloves in a slow, dreamy sort of way. Peter took this to be a signal that she wouldn't mind if he were to hold her hand, or even both her hands. He was right. Sitting forward more, in facing her, he was able to take both her hands.

No kiss yet. Far too early. They simply gazed at each other in joyful incredulity.

How many would-be lovers have behaved in this way? We shall never know. No more words were uttered for quite some time except "Oh, Timothea" and "Oh, Peter."

But there is one crystal-cold fact which we do need to know. Believe it or not, this was actually the very first time these two lovers had made any physical contact of any kind.

Whether this situation is unprecedented or commonplace, we are now to be allowed to find out the reasons for it.

Timothea Gudgeon was the first to take the further initiative. She gave Peter Smith's hands a little shake, signalling that she wanted her own to be released. He released them. She then simply folded back the fold-up arm-rest which was beside her. He got the new signal. He was beside her in a flash. But still there was to be no kiss.

Nestling up against him, encircled by his arm, she was the picture of childhood innocence. Cynics may not agree, but there was not a hint of any prurience in this particular railway-carriage.

"Peter," said Timothea, "I have to tell you one or two things. My surname is my unmarried name. I reverted to it after my husband and I divorced. Reverted, I hope, with a little more wisdom."

"We could all do with a little more wisdom," Peter reminiscently sighed.

"But twenty-two years, Peter! Why did it have to take us twenty-two years to learn a little more wisdom?"

"Actually, now that I've seen you again, it doesn't really seem all that long ago. It feels like just a few weeks."

"It feels like that to me, too. But the fact remains. We've wasted twenty-two years."

"It's an old, old problem, Timothea. We're not the only ones. I'm not much gone on poetry, but I did come across one old English poem which sums it all up so beautifully. One line of it has gone through my head over and over again," and Peter quoted it sadly but smilingly. "I did but see her passing by, yet I shall love her till I die."

Timothea wriggled out of his arm in playful reproach. "I know the poem. It's a bit unfair, don't you think?"

Equally playfully: "I certainly don't think it unfair in any way at all!"

"Peter, it wasn't me who did the passing by. It was you."

"Me?"

"I was on the beach, wasn't I? On my rug, wasn't I? Flaunting myself in my bikini, wasn't I? In other words, posing like mad."

"Well, yes. That's very true. Rather a new and too shocking a sight for dear old Southwold."

"Peter, I had only been there ten minutes when you came walking past."

Dreamily said: "On that beautifully simple promenade. With that line of bathing-huts …"

"Peter, that's exactly right. Blue blazer. White trousers. Dazzlingly white trousers. No hat, though."

"I still have that blazer."

"Peter, you did stop and look at me. I grant you that. But it was only for a moment."

"And what a moment!"

"Peter, I sat up as soon as I saw you. We looked at each other. We knew it immediately, didn't we?"

"Timothea, we did. We knew it immediately. I'd never had that kind of feeling ever before. And I was never to have it again – until today."

"But Peter, you walked on! You passed on by! You were only a few yards away. Why couldn't you have come closer? We could have spoken."

A big sigh from Peter. He said carefully: "Well, you see, I was on holiday there with my then wife."

"As I was," cried Timothea, "with my then fiancé! But he was sleeping off a hangover at the hotel. You could easily have chatted me up."

Their conversation was becoming a bit of a tiff. But it was only a playful tiff. They were enjoying it. A shade more seriously, Timothea moved away and said: "Your then wife? Any children?"

"Thankfully not. I like children, but couples who should never have got married should never, in my opinion, have children."

A rueful sigh from Timothea. "I know what you mean, old boy. I did try to fall in love with other men, but it never worked. Never worked with my husband either."

"Let's avoid all talk of past mistakes. But this complaint of yours about my passing by is most unjust. My then wife didn't like Southwold. She wanted to get away and was waiting for me, in the car. I just went back to to have a last look at the sea, that's all."

"That's no argument!"

"Yes it is. When I got to the car, I found she'd gone off to buy cigarettes or something. So I went back, Timothea! You had gone. Gone!"

Jokingly aghast, Timothea cried "Forgive me!" and was quickly back in the seated embrace of Peter's arm. (Still no kiss.) She explained: "I'd rushed back to the hotel to change and go off in search. I described the white trousers, but no one knew anything about them. Stupidly, I got married. Had to go off with my husband to Canada – for fifteen years."

"This morning," Peter ventured to murmur into her hair, "my taxi-driver saw that I was miserable."

"Oh, dear! About me?"

"I had separate reasons for being a bit glum. But this is the point I'm making. He might only have been trying to cheer me up. But he did accurately predict that today was going to be My Lucky Day. May I dare to hope that you, as well, will always think think of it as your own lucky day?"

"Of course," she said, but, to his surprise, moving away from him with a slight frown. "Peter, if anything ever delays you or goes somehow wrong, will you do your best to get in touch?"

Mildly reproachful, he said: "Doesn't that go without saying?"

"If you can't phone, would you write me a letter? I can't bear the thought of perhaps not hearing from you. I'll give you my address and phone number."

She took a pair of extraordinarily black-rimmed glasses from her handbag. Oddly, to Peter, they enhanced her beautiful eyes and made her look strongly efficient. But attractively efficient. Finishing, she took them off and gave him the piece of paper. The writing on it was, for him, immediately characteristic of her. Stunningly so.

A more staggering surprise: "And you live in Stratford-on-

Avon! That's no great distance from my cottage. How long have you lived there?"

"Just three months. I didn't know the area, but I was working in London for a year after I got back from Canada. By chance, I saw an ad for a senior receptionist. I didn't much like the hotel in London. I somehow knew I'd get this new job. So much better."

"All this," said Peter, laughing and trembling in highly flustered satisfaction, "is so incredibly coincidental as to be magical."

"I was even able to find myself a nice little flat not too far away." She said this in quite a dulled voice and was wringing her fingers slightly. "It's only a furnished service-flat, but I'm happy there."

Peter now noticed that Timothea didn't seem to be sharing his excitement. Being, as we know, a bit naïve, he simply assumed that she needed to be wooed a little more assiduously. After all, he was thinking to himself, all women are still women. They can't resist playing hard-to-get, can they? And isn't it a fact that ducks and drakes in every public park illustrate the same trait? And peahens and peacocks at stately homes open to the public?

It was ever thus.

Sitting slightly apart from him, she said: "Why did the taxi-driver need to reassure you? What was making you so especially miserable?"

Cheerfully: "Oh, only for very boring reasons! I love popping down to London for a day or two. But not when I'm compelled to cross swords with my ex-wife's vile solicitor."

"Being difficult, is he?"

"Oh, only for the past seventeen years!"

"Peter, I'm sorry you've got this problem. You don't hate your ex-wife, do you?"

"Actually, no. I was always hoping she would marry and find happiness. But she seems to prefer a single life. We've not actually communicated for years, not even by phone."

"Was she in love with you?"

"I doubt if she knew what being in love really meant. She was a simple, rather dull-minded person I'm sorry to say. We should never have married."

"Peter, I feel the same way about my ex-husband."

"But I don't suppose," he said, still cheerfully but not quite so cheerfully, "that your solicitor soaks him for ever-increasing maintenance?"

"I only took what I needed when our little boy had to be looked after. Only the one child. He's still young, of course, but legally grown up."

Something in her tone made him ask: "Turned out all right, has he?"

"Oh, yes. Very bright future. But what's the right word? He's becoming more and more pedantic."

"Young men are often pedantic."

"For instance, I mustn't say Stratford-on-Avon. I have to say Stratford *upon* Avon. He's discovered that's the right way of saying it."

Fully cheerful again: "I'll have to remember that if I meet him."

Timothea urgently seized Peter's hand. "Peter, that's what worries me. He's meeting me at Paddington."

Peter was quick to catch her drift. "And you'd prefer me to hang back a bit?"

"More than a bit, I'm sorry to say. He doesn't like men paying me attention."

"Oh, dear!"

"Also, he's trying to get me to go back to Canada where he works. And where his father is."

Peter blinked quite a bit over this piece of information. He blinked still more when she added: "My son doesn't like me using my unmarried name. And I refuse to go back. Oh, Peter!"

Peter was about to enclose her in his arms, but he was interrupted.

"Tickets, please."

A uniformed ticket-inspector had entered. His hand-held ticket-clipper was at the ready. He was of late middle-age but was so crouch-like that he seemed much older.

Peter was able to produce his ticket, Timothea was not. Agitatedly, she rooted in her bag but was immediately forgiven.

"Have this one on us," said the ticket-inspector, "if you've lost it – or even didn't buy it. Bless your two hearts. Let's just see to it that you stays private-like," and he slapped an adhesive label on the compartment window. (The words on it were: "No entry. Compartment Reserved.")

"By God," he muttered to himself, "now I know what I've really missed in life," and he went out firmly and quickly.

There had been no time to thank him and he didn't appear to want to be thanked. Timothea was close to happy tears over his words.

Peter was just as affected, but he was more controlled. He remained silent until Timothea said: "Have you ever been with the Milk Marketing Board?"

Peter was staggered by this question. "Me? Milk Marketing Board? I've never been with the Milk Marketing Board."

"It's something I heard in Southwold. I was trying to describe you. A waitress said you sounded like a very good-looking young man she fancied for herself. Didn't get his name. But he did tell her he was with the Milk Marketing Board."

"Timothea, I have to disappoint you. I was not that man."

Happy again, Timothea said: "You've dashed all my hopes. What could possibly be more attractive, in a man, than to be with the Milk Marketing Board?"

"I can only tell you, regretfully, that I was working as a lecturer at the trade-technical institute when I passed you by in Southwold."

"And how much lower have you sunk now?"

"Actually, I'm still with the same dreary old institute in Woodley Norton. The only difference is that I'm now the deputy-principal. I'll be totally in charge in one year's time. But I'll still be lecturing."

"What tedious, dry-as-dust subjects do you lecture upon?"

"The term lecturer is, perhaps, one which your son might describe as untrue to its academic connotation. I am more of a demonstrator. I teach woodwork and joinery. What's even worse, I enjoy what I do. I love woodwork. It's even my hobby. In no way am I a man of taste and culture."

"Peter," said Timothea, "you really are the man for me," and they both went on in this way, joking at each other's expense, for quite some time.

Peter had not been worried by Timothea's revelation about her son. Peter was accustomed to coping with young adults. Nevertheless, he respected her sudden return to the subject at this point. Cheerfully, he promised not to make himself known "just yet."

"How long," he asked, in all innocence, "will you be away from Stratford *upon* Avon?"

To his surprise, although he had agreed to be tactful about the pedantic son, Timothea's unease was renewed.

"My son has come over from Canada on his own," she haltingly said. "He and I will be staying in London for a couple of days. Then we go off up to the Lake District to stay with my sister Molly and her rather elderly husband."

"You get on with them all right?"

"Of course I do," she rather sharply said.

"Timothea," he affably said, "I'm only asking how long you will be away."

"Fourteen days," she said, looking apologetic for having spoken sharply. "Peter, do please forgive me. I have some problems. The hotel has given me two weeks off before I'm even entitled to them. Very nice people. They like me. But please don't try to contact me until I'm back in Stratford."

"As you wish," he smilingly shrugged.

"Peter," she was anxiously quick to say, "I'll try to phone you tomorrow – or even tonight if I can. It's amazing how difficult it is to make a discreet phone-call. Where exactly will you be today?"

"It's called the Golconda Hotel, just off Russell Square in Bloomsbury. I always stay there when I pop down to London," and he enthusiastically gave her the phone-number as well as the address and phone-number of his cottage – and even the number for his office in the Woodley Norton Trade-Technical.

At this point, familiar as he was with the suburban approach to Paddington, Peter was genuinely shocked at suddenly seeing it.

"We're nearly in," he cried, jumping up. "I quite thought we were to be allowed to go on for ever!"

"So did I," said Timothea, rising and putting on her gloves, her matching gloves.

Peter turned away from the window. He stood facing her. For both of them, the train was making no sound whatsoever. The compartment seemed to be beyond all space and time, a quite ridiculous form of delusion surely? But, no matter what we think of it, this was the moment for the most valued kiss of all time. It was valued not only for being, in itself, a proposal of marriage. It was a moment for Peter and Timothea when they felt the spirit of undying love possessing them.

Peter had never before experienced the deep thrill of such a kiss and nor had Timothea.

He only needed to breathe the traditional question and she only needed to breathe her reply. But she was the first to become more audible.

She whispered: "I did but see *him* passing by, yet I shall love *him* till I die."

The train had stopped. It had arrived at Paddington station. Outside the window was an increasing and bustling crowd, but the interior of that compartment had the venerable stillness and calm of a deserted museum.

"I think," said Peter, "that we'd better get off."

"Oh, that poor old chap," said Timothea, and she was referring to the humane ticket-inspector.

Peter knew what she meant. Theirs had been the moment, the one precious moment of all time, the moment which the ticket-inspector had known would soon be theirs and which had never been his. Peter was thinking: "That chap could have been me."

"Today," said Timothea, happy but shivering and her voice trembling, "really has been my lucky day. Oh, Peter, how I wish we could both go to that hotel of yours! I don't want to be with anyone else but you."

In helping her out of the train, Peter made a consoling little joke about the twenty-two years they wouldn't have to endure again. Both were now very fond of the train, even the terrible corridor – as narrow as a Dickensian chimney-flue.

She turned to him after they alighted, and the turn was so tenderly loving that he couldn't resist kissing her again. Just a quick departure-kiss. But he again thrilled head-to-toe; and he again noticed that her very breath had the fragrance of cottage flowers, his cottage, his flowers.

"Oh, there's Molly," she broke off to say, "my sister! I didn't know *she* would turn up!"

Pausing only long enough to add: "Don't forget your coat and your suitcase. You've left them on the train. I must go. Goodbye for now, dear lovely Peter," and off she went, through the dispersing throng and waving to attract her sister's attention.

"Not much trouble there," Peter was thinking, and he was pleasantly puzzled. He could see what appeared to be a three-person reception-committee. One was a frowning and rather stout young man, obviously the pedantic son; but the sister was a merry-looking person who was soon waving back at Timothea. The third person was a perfectly contented-looking woman.

Peter didn't fully understand Timothea's previous agitation, but he accepted that his engagement might be construed as a trifle odd. Even the most tolerant of one's relations, as he knew from his own, had to be tactfully handled. Ecstatically obedient in fulfilling Timothea's reminder, he was back on the train in seconds.

He was already chortling at the prospect of associating with the merry Molly. All Timothea's other relations, he was sure, would be just as wonderful. With his heart beating excitedly, he stayed in the compartment only long enough to venerate every single feature Timothea had seen or touched. (This included the arm-rest she had encouragingly folded back. He lovingly returned it to its formal position.)

Leaving the carriage and after quietly closing the door, he made for the Underground. Timothea and her reception-committee had, of course, vanished, but he did look around for any sign of them. In looking at all the people milling around, he was thinking: "What a wonderful world it would be if everyone were to be in love as much as I am! No more nastiness, no more wars."

He was on his way to Russell Square and a late lunch at the Golconda, but, even on the totally disinterested Underground, he was bursting to tell everyone of his good fortune. He was restrained only by a rather sheepish thought. Wouldn't a man of fifty be regarded as a bit of an old fool for being so much in love?

Emerging from the tube-station for Russell Square, he felt the same previous affection he had always felt for this part of London. But, this time, it was enhanced by his love for Timothea. It was such a private feeling of bliss that he believed no one else could possibly have experienced it. With his suitcase in one hand and with his raincoat over his other arm – and, of course, in his fetching trilby – he felt he was treading the pastures of heaven in sauntering up to the Golconda Hotel.

He actually murmured aloud the words: "I really am the luckiest man in all the world!"

And perhaps he was – together with all the other people who have experienced this same feeling. But would they have all been quite so unmindful of the fact, as Peter was, that London was changing? That the entire country was changing?

This was the period in time when Mrs Thatcher was still on her political throne. Her crown had only been knocked slightly askew.

Peter, we have to sadly say (if we are sad about that sort of thing) had absolutely no interest in metropolitan politics. The only newspaper he ever read was the *Banbury Guardian* and that only when he remembered to buy it.

CHAPTER TWO

Very Peculiar Behaviour

If that train from Woodley Norton to London is to be described as antiquated, then the Golconda Hotel in Bloomsbury must also be so described.

It had no televison anywhere on the premises. It did have a radio in the lounge, but this was part of an old wooden radiogram and seldom switched on. In fairness to the lack of modern facilities, we have to accept that few of the guests needed to make any use of them. The hotel was primarily for provincial guests wanting a "moderately-priced basis" for excursions to theatres, the British Museum and the National Gallery.

These guests were usually aged between fifty and eighty (and sometimes beyond). Peter Smith, therefore, was suitable for this age-bracket, but, unusually, he had been using the place ever since he began work after leaving school. Just two jobs. First, in London, then, at the age of twenty-six, at the trade-technical in Oxfordshire.

It was, of course, a vegetarian hotel.

Yes, Peter was that most eccentric of persons, a vegetarian. And he loved that hotel. Yes, loved it. But even meat-eaters would admit that the cooking was excellent and that good wine was served in the quiet cleanliness and tinkle of the restaurant.

Another good point was (not always found even in certain hotels of today) that every room had a telephone. All phone-calls were routed through a "modernised" contraption known as a PBX (private branch exchange) and strictly controlled by Mrs Collop. She was the hitherto steadfast owner and manageress.

"Peter," she said, buttonholing him in the hall after his lunch, "may I just see you in my office? On a matter of confidential importance?"

Still feeling lovingly charitable towards the whole world, Peter grandly said: "Certainly, my dear old girl!"

In the presence of the PBX and a heavily old Remington typewriter, Mrs Collop sat him down and wagged a finger.

"Peter, promise me you'll keep this under your hat."

"I promise."

"I don't want any of my other guests to be upset. You, I know, will take the news well. Peter, I'm going to retire. I'm parting with the Golconda."

"Oh, dear," he said, far too happy really to care a pin. "I do hope it won't be taken over by a bunch of modern-day carnivores."

"That won't be within my control. But Peter," and here she spoke more dramatically, "I'm going to give you the recipe."

"Good heavens," he cried, genuinely suprised, "the recipe?"

For many years, many guests (and including errant meat-eaters) had pleaded with Mrs Collop to reveal the secret of her special dish – an absolutely scrumptious savoury. Each one was cooked in a separate tin and looked like a little round cake. She had always refused to divulge.

"I'm especially fond of you, Peter."

"I know that, Mrs Collop. Thank you."

"Before I give you the recipe, I want you to promise that you'll never reveal it to anyone."

"That's a promise I can easily make. I have many secrets."

"You appreciate what this means? You'll always have to be the one who cooks it."

"Oh," he said, almost carelessly, "I do all my own cooking. If I don't feel like doing it, I just go out somewhere."

"How typical," said Mrs Collop, a little sternly, "of one of nature's true bachelors!"

Peter was still seeing, in his mind's eye, Timothea's enchanting lips and the way they were parted slightly in repose. And her surely perfectly-shaped ear when she turned her head.

"My God," he muttered, but Mrs Collop didn't notice his thrillingly faraway anticipations.

She presented the recipe. It had been typed out with her own fingers on the heavy Remington, with much use of the red section of the ribbon.

"Thank you, Mrs Collop," and for some moments Peter could only sit pretending to read it.

"Even if you re-marry, which I very much doubt," Mrs Collop went on to say, "you mustn't even tell your wife. I mean it, Peter."

"Very much doubt? What on earth do you mean by that?" Peter was joyfully amused. He would have spoken of his own news had she not gone on to be even more stern.

"I'm not quite old enough to be your mother," she said, wagging the finger again, "but I feel motherly towards you."

"That's always been a comfort, Mrs Collop."

"I wouldn't like to hear of you making the same mistake twice."

"I'm not likely to make such a mistake again, Mrs Collop."

"I'm glad to hear you say so," said Mrs Collop, completely misunderstanding him. "You are not born to be a married man. You are a natural bachelor. It was inevitable that you would cause your poor wife so much unnecessary suffering."

"My poor wife, you say?"

"It's such a pity she's never felt able to come here ever again. She loved the Golconda."

Peter was too good-humoured a man to feel any angry indignation, but this last statement made him leap to his feet.

Waving the recipe, he said: "She hated the Golconda. She didn't even like this wonderful dish of yours! I had thought she would like it. That's why I brought her here, just after we were married. She hated anything with lentils."

Mrs Collop nearly fainted.

"But I could have got so fond of her," she wailed. "I've never forgotten how nice she was!"

"She was a confirmed meat-eater," said Peter, "and that was just one of many reasons for our incompatibility. I'm sorry to have upset you like this. Would you like me to get you a cup of tea?"

"I'm all right, thank you Peter."

Poor old girl, thought Peter, she really did look shatteringly disillusioned.

"Thank you again for giving me this recipe. I will treasure it. I will observe your conditions. Meanwhile, might I ask a separate favour of you?"

"I always do my best," sniffed Mrs Collop, "to serve all my guests to the best of my ability."

"I know that, Mrs Collop. I'm expecting a phone-call. If I'm out, will you very kindly take a message and leave it in my room?"

"Yes, Mr Smith," said Mrs Collop more than a shade formally. "Will you be in for the evening meal?"

"Oh, indeed! But I have to go out now, to Russell Square. I did mean to go to Clerkenwell, to see my ex-wife's solicitor. But I've cancelled that. I'm seeing my own solicitor instead. I'm going to put my foot down, you see, pretty firmly."

"I don't quite know what you're talking about, Mr Smith."

"I'll tell you more a bit later on."

Mrs Collop brightened up. "Thank you, Peter. You've always been a good boy really."

It says something for Peter's mood that he left the office but dashed back to it very like a boy. The PBX had broken into life. But the high-pitched buzz (the signal for an incoming call) was a disappointment (for Peter).

He left the hotel and walked along the street and into Russell Square – in glorious sunshine – with some anxiety about Timothea's possible taste in food. After all, he knew very little about her. Could it turn out that she, too, wouldn't appreciate the Golconda Rissole? What if she were to be another enthusiastic eater of once-living flesh?

Peter was able to dismiss these fastidious thoughts in the very next second.

He did so by uttering an age-old sentence which, of course, he thought he was the only one to utter. ("Oh, we can work something out!")

Dodging the encircling traffic imperfectly, he bounded across the road and into the square's central garden. (Note that, please. It is called a garden, not an "open space.") Peter had always been very fond of this garden. Many an open-air lunch he had taken there, with his great friend Ralph. He was now making a short cut, across the square, to the line of 19th century terraced houses on the far side.

One of these houses, actually quite narrow, was not as elegant and as spacious within as the façade suggested. Peter was soon facing Ralph in a cramped office on the first floor. They were both beaming with pleasure at the sight of each other, but Ralph was introducing his recently acquired secretary. He was being rather sheepish about her. She was aloofly young and aloofly attractive. She herself cut short the introduction and said: "Excuse me, sir, but I have other things to get on with."

"Oh, yes – of course! But Anna, do let me just say that Mr Smith is my oldest friend. In the days when we shared these premises with the editorial staff of the Truss-Fitter's Gazette, Peter was then their glorified office-boy."

"He means," Peter explained, "that I was a junior staff-writer on a magazine known as the *Cabinet-Maker's Monthly*. Defunct now, alas."

"It was his first job," said Ralph, "but he eventually got the sack."

"These are foul slanders," said Peter. "I only left to take up a lecturing appointment in the Woodley Norton Trade Technical."

"An institute," said Ralph. "Cold and dark."

"As for this man," said Peter, "he only just escaped being thrown out of university. How on earth he managed to get taken on here is still a mystery."

"Don't listen to him, Anna," said Ralph, jokily but a bit nervously.

The young lady so addressed showed not a flicker of interest.

She coolly said to the slightly cringing Ralph: "Sir, did I ever give you permission to address me as Anna?"

"Er, no," he said.

"That being the case, sir, please address me in future in a proper manner."

"Yes, Miss Yosenhants."

"Have I made myself sufficiently clear?"

"Yes, Miss Yosenhants. I do beg your pardon."

Miss Yosenhants went out, and Ralph sighed in genuine sadness. He said: "That's why, behind her back, we call her Miss Frozen Pants."

Peter, still in his euphoric state, mildly said: "That's in very bad taste, old chap."

"I know," Ralph gloomily said. "She's a lovely girl. Super-intelligent, actually. I secretly adore her. All the men do."

Ralph, who liked his name to be pronounced "Rafe," was bothered on another matter. He sat back behind his desk, stiffly fidgety. He drew a deep breath and abruptly said: "Peter, I have to be very serious with you. I'm hoping you'll take it in good part."

"Anything you say, old boy, is all right with me. You know that, surely?"

"I do indeed. But I've been evading this matter in every interview for the past two years – just as I did just now! Fancy trying to get a smile out of Frozen Pants! Evading the matter yet again! What a waste of my professional time!"

"Rafe," said Peter, in his kindliest tone, "do please just say what you mean."

"That's the point, you see – my professional time. We've had another Partners' Meeting and I'm being criticised. We're getting top-notch here. We're bursting at the seams. Soon be moving," and he finally said, in a rush: "Peter, we can no longer accord you concessionary fees!"

He fell back in his office-chair and shut his eyes as if tired. Although the same age as Peter, he did look tired and, we have to say, older.

"Rafe, old chap," said Peter, "we can surely still be friends if I engage a solicitor a bit nearer home?"

Rafe opened his eyes and smiled a simply enormous smile. "But of course, old boy! It's what I've been getting at! A good country sole-solicitor could handle your troubles at a lower fee than I would have to charge," and he leapt up to shake Peter's hand energetically. "It's been a long time, our friendship. Ever since we both started work in this old dump. I do have regrets about all this. But we'll still see a lot of each other, won't we?"

"Not only that, old chap, I'm hoping you'll be my best man."

Peter was not above guile in springing a surprise of this sort. He openly grinned as his startled friend rose from his chair behind the desk.

"Best man, you say?" Rafe spoke in delighted incredulity. "You mean you're going to marry? Again? In spite of previous experience?"

"It's my main reason for popping in to see you. Marriage invalidates an existing will, I've remembered you saying. I was rather hoping you would draft something to accomodate my troubles."

"Oh, never mind about all that," said Rafe, exploding with pleasure. He came out from behind his desk to pump Peter's hand in the heartiest of all hand-shakes. "By God, this calls for at least a token form of emergency celebration."

With both of these friends chortling madly, Rafe was producing two glasses and a decanter of sherry when Miss Yosenhants opened the door.

"Sir," she said, in her coolest voice, "the other partners have foregathered in the attic room. Tea has already been served. They are expecting you, sir."

"For heaven's sake, Miss Yosenhants, one of my dearest friends has just told me he's going to get spliced! I'll be there in a few minutes."

Miss Yosenhants withdrew without a word and with her brow smoothly unclouded.

In a sudden spurt of anger, Rafe yelled: "Yes and next time try knocking the door before you come in," but, in the next second, he added: "I hope she didn't hear that. Still, here we go! Bless your wicked old heart, dearest Peter, and may you have all the love and happiness you've been missing."

After this sincere emergency-toast, Peter sat down on a client-chair and continued to chortle. Rafe also sat down to chortle, except for being seated on the front edge of his desk.

What more wonderful a scene could there be? Two old friends talking about love!

"Peter, dear boy, do you mind if I ask? Has this been a case of love at first sight?"

"It has indeed," said Peter, who was now glowing with unrestrained happiness.

"Where did you first see the lady?"

"On the beach at Southwold. I was walking along that beautifully simple promenade. She was on the beach. I looked at her. She looked at me. And that was it – we were in love."

"Oh, you lucky devil! Not a word to Lizzie about this, but I have never known love at first sight. I've longed to have that experience, but it's never happened."

"Not even with Lizzie?"

"Not even with Lizzie whom I love. But it's not romantic love. She's nice to be with, and all that, but I don't thrill to the marrow. You, presumably, do thrill to the marrow?"

"Yes, at the very sight of Timothea, I do thrill to the marrow. An almost constant state."

"Timothea? Oh, what a lovely name! I can't wait to meet her. Might I just ask? How old is she?"

"Forty-five."

Rafe's expression now became an odd mixture of both relief and disappointment. He got off the desk to say: "I shouldn't have imagined too young a girl – as I'm afraid I did. But forty-five seems a bit too old to inspire love at first sight. I beg your pardon, old boy. Am I wrong?"

"I don't know if you're wrong. I didn't fall in love with her at that age."

"But you've just told me you did!"

"Listen carefully. I fell in love with her when she was twenty-three. She was wearing a bikini."

"On the beach at Southwold?"

"Correct. You've twigged."

Rafe paced his office in agitation, then wheeled round on Peter to say: "What I haven't twigged, you ghastly man, is how and why you've kept this relationship a secret all these years. It's very peculiar behaviour on your part."

"You've got it all wrong, you idiot."

"Deceiving us all! Even Lizzie, poor little Lizzie, one of your greatest fans! Oh, what a skunk!"

"Listen, you absolute moron. After seeing her on the beach at Southwold, I never saw her again until this morning."

"This morning?" shrieked Rafe.

"Yes, twenty-two years later. On the train."

"On the train? This morning?"

"The train into Paddington. She was on the train when I got in at Woodley Norton."

"Peter, I am befuddled. I admit it. When did you actually propose to this wench?"

"On the train."

"On the train?" Rafe again shrieked. "You are either pulling my leg or you're completely mad. Which is it?"

"Neither. I was on the train and that's where I proposed and where she accepted."

Rafe sank down in his chair behind the desk. "What did the other passengers think of all this?"

"There weren't any other passengers."

"What!"

"Well, not in our compartment. There may have been a few elsewhere on the train. We were alone. It was all very strange in some ways."

"You can say that again," Rafe almost yelled. But he recovered himself and sat forward looking wistfully concerned. "Forgive me, Peter. A woman of forty-five can be jolly attractive these days. They can even give birth up to the age of fifty – and even over."

"I'm not yet thinking along those lines, thank you. But I'll tell you this, old sport. She doesn't seem to me to have changed all that much," and, playing with his hat, he gazed into visionary nothingness. "I still sort of see her as when I first saw her on that beach. It's a picture I've sort of cherished for a long, long time…"

Tenderly spoken by Rafe: "And does she think about you in the same way?"

"She does, yes. It's quite uncanny. We seem to think and feel in the same way as each other."

"Oh, you lucky old dog," sighed Rafe. "I can't wait to see her. And of course I would love to be your Best Man. Just as a matter of slight interest, what church might the wedding be at?"

"That's not yet been discussed."

"What's her religion? If any?"

"I don't know."

"Peter, are you being wise? To propose to a woman on a train when you don't really know much about her could be a bit – well, downright foolish. I'm still your lawyer for at least another two minutes. I must advise you to be cautious. Is she, for instance, a cranky vegetarian like yourself?"

"That I don't know either."

"Oh my God," cried Rafe bluntly. "I'm beginning to think you really are bonkers!"

"She did tell me one or two important sort of things. Her address, for instance. She lives in Stratford-Upon-Avon."

"Stratford-on-Avon, eh? Nice place."

"Stratford upon Avon. Get it right, you ignoramus."

Peter got to his feet, still playing with his hat. He beamingly added: "I'd better be going. But let me advise you, me old sport. Heed Miss Yosenhants. Secretaries must always be obeyed. I have one myself. She's pure gold."

It was at this exact point that Miss Yosenhants re-entered – again without knocking. She came gliding in and stood holding the door wide open, her hand on the historically surviving china knob.

"Sir," she said, in her coldest tone yet, "tea has already been served and the partners are waiting. Upstairs, sir. In the attic room, sir."

"All right," said Rafe, but a shade mutinously. To Peter, he said: "When will you next be seeing your Timothea?"

"In about two weeks. She was on the train because she was going on holiday to the Lake District. Her sister, it seems, lives there."

"Jolly nice place. Tell you what, old boy. I hope you'll pop round to us tonight. Have a spot of dinner, eh? Lizzie will be mad keen to interrogate you."

"Thanks, old boy, but another time if you don't mind. I need to stay in tonight. At the Golconda. I'm expecting a call from Timothea. It's bound to be tonight, I think."

"I quite understand, old boy," and Rafe slapped Peter on the back in the old-boy manner.

"Tea," said Miss Yosenhants warningly.

"Yes, Miss Yosenhants, said Rafe, but he paused in the doorway. He turned, struck by a new thought.

"I say, old boy, there's one thing that really puzzles me. That line is always packed when Lizzie and I come to see you. Why was the train so empty when you were on it with this Timothea of yours?"

"I've no idea," said Peter, still beaming with contentment. "Frankly, I would have been happy to let it go puffing and chuff-chuffing on for ever – for ever!"

The effect of this simple-minded statement upon Rafe was strong. He actually went pale. He seized Peter by the arm and said: "What sort of rot have you been telling me? Puffing and chuffing?"

"Well, yes. Puffing and chuffing."

"Peter, you've not been telling me the truth."

Astounded by this accusation, Peter said: "But I have, old boy. All steam-trains puff and chuff."

Rafe compressed his lips for a moment in what appeared to be trembling anger. He then said: "Peter, the last steam-train to run on British Rail was in 1968. That's thirteen years ago."

Peter tried to make light of this statement by saying: "I can only assure you, my dear old boy, that Timothea and I arrived in Paddington on a chuff-chuff. I know little about trains, but it *was* a chuff-chuff."

"Furthermore," said Rafe, in a lawyer-like voice, "the last steam-train out of Paddington itself was even earlier. Sixteen years ago. I myself was on that train to your part of the world, with Lizzie. Are you even sure that it was Paddington you arrived at?"

Without waiting for a reply, Rafe bolted off through the outer office without even looking back. Peter was left looking more puzzled than worried. Surely this was just Rafe being a bit daft? He looked at the cool Miss Yosenhants. She was standing still, expressionless. As for the altercation, it had attracted no attention from in the outer office. That nice big room was stuffed with legal people busily occupied at separate desks. The intensive bustle reminded Peter of the editorial room on the ground floor where he had worked in his youth. He was reminded, too, of how he had chummed up with Rafe and, with him, bought sandwiches from Jolly's sandwich-bar.

Miss Yosenhants said to him, in her cool voice: "I'll show you out, Mr Smith. This way, please."

"Oh no," he politely said, putting on his hat, "I can see myself out. I do know these premises. I mustn't waste your time. Nice to have met you. Good afternoon."

"You're not wasting my time," she said, in a lowered and urgent voice. "I need to speak to you privately. This way, please," she added more loudly.

Peter instantly took his hat off and she led him along to the head of the staircase.

They descended in silence and, in Peter's case, in some confusion. Why on earth, he was thinking, had his friend been so cross with him?

CHAPTER THREE

Honey From The Meadow-Bees

I

Once outside the front door and on the pavement, Peter politely said: "Thank you for seeing me out, Miss Yosenhants. Nice to have met you. Good afternoon," and he put on his hat and began to walk off.

To his surprise and even mild shock, Miss Yosenhants gripped him by the arm and restrained him. She said: "Didn't you hear what I told you? I need to speak to you privately."

"I'm so sorry," was all he could think of as a reply. "I'm a bit woolly today."

After a quick look to left and right, like a conscientious nursemaid, she piloted him across the road and towards a distant bench in the Square's ample centre-garden.

"Sit down, please" she said, and he complied somewhat ditheringly. His dreamy visions of Timothea and his anxieties about Rafe would have been too heady a mixture even for a teenager, let alone a man of fifty.

Miss Yosenhants, in being seated beside him, was half-turned towards him. She looked closely into his face and, to his fresh surprise, began to grin. The grin became a laugh. In seconds, the laugh was almost uncontrollable.

"Oh dear me," she said, recovering, "there really is nothing so funny as men when they fall for the classical-secretary act."

Light dawned upon Peter. "You mean this disdainful manner of yours is just an act?"

"Of course it is! It's one of the skills."

"I can't see how being disdainful to people as nice as poor old Rafe can be described as one of the skills." Peter felt really shocked. "You can't surely be serious?"

"Mr Smith," she said, becoming indeed strongly serious, "there is nothing your friend needs more, at the moment, than the classical-secretary act. It helps to keep him balanced and secure."

"Miss Yosenhants, I don't think I can approve of what you're saying."

"No? Perhaps you might approve more if I say that you, Mr Smith, are a good friend to my boss. I think you are the best friend he could possibly have. If I may so, I instantly detected this."

Peter raised his eyebrows considerably. "It's a nice compliment. Thank you. But why are you saying these things about Rafe?"

"Because, as a good friend, you need to understand him a lot better than you do. Why do you think he was upset over the matter of the train you travelled on?"

"I've no idea, I must admit."

"It's an interesting little train mystery which, I'm sure, could be easily explained. It is the reaction of my boss that is by far the most important aspect of it."

"I still don't see what you mean. Shouldn't you be getting back to work?" and Peter stood up.

"Sit down," she said, and he sat down.

"Like many amusing people with a really kindly sense of humour, my boss has hidden problems. They cause him real distress. This, perhaps, is a time in your life when you need to understand this more clearly."

"What facts do you have which bear out what you're saying?"

"One fact, Mr Smith, is that your former wife has been

phoning up my boss. She's been pestering him, on and off, for some eighteen months."

"Pestering him, you say?"

"I've only been his secretary for just over three months, but I've read the file. Furthermore, even in my tenure to date, she has phoned our offices three times. I've intercepted two of those calls myself. I may well suggest an injunction."

"Good heavens! I had no idea …"

"Of course you've had no idea. My boss has kept it from you. He doesn't want you to be upset. But he knows exactly what she's up to. She wants to destroy your friendship with him."

"My goodness me," Peter said, hardly able to comprehend this news. "What's my friendship with Rafe got to do with an ex-wife I hardly speak to?"

"She an evil woman, Peter. Or close to evil. I can't say, obviously how evil she can become in the future. But you really do need to watch out."

"Thank you for the warning, Anna," said Peter, also dropping the formality over names. "As I say, I hardly ever speak to her – not even on the phone."

"She's probably a woman who works obliquely in destroying the lives of people she hates. I wouldn't mind betting she's gone behind your back and phoned up that institute of yours."

"I've always been aware of her sly and nasty solicitor, but I never realised she's been phoning up you lot in Russell Square. I can't believe it. It's too ridiculously awful to be true. She was never as bad as all that, I do assure you."

Anna Yosenhants stood up. She said: "No matter how ridiculous and awful it may sound, it's stone-cold truth. She's poison. Simple as that. I must get back to my office."

Peter was so shocked that he remained seated. He had never met a woman like Anna before. He was thinking: "Is she some sort of nut-case? Poor old Elsie can't have become as bad as all this! It's too unbelievable."

Anna said: "Let me give you my card," and she handed it to him from her handbag. "Any time you think you might need my help, such as it is, do get in touch. Phone me at my flat."

"Thank you, Anna," and he stood up and issued an invitation without knowing why. "Look here, would you care to join me for lunch tomorrow?"

"Tomorrow being Friday," she said, now having become pleasingly friendly, "I can easily do so. Thank you very much, I'd love to do so! My boss goes off to Brussels tomorrow and I do not. I'm giving him a bit of a respite. I've got my own secretary to go with him. She needs the tedious experience. It will do her good. Improve her French."

"You have a secretary yourself?"

"Of course I have. All top secretaries have secretaries. Where do we lunch?"

"At the Golconda, I would suggest. Have you heard of it?"

"Well, yes," she said, rather hesitatingly.

"One o'clock, then, if that's all right. I'm on my annual leave, you see. I was going to stay quite a few days in London, but I think it would be best if I go home. Probably on Saturday."

"Sure you're all right?" she asked.

He said he was "all right" and she went off – back across the square. But Peter sat down and remained on the bench for quite some time.

"By God," he was thinking, "what a day!"

He kept saying "what a day" all the way back to his room at the Golconda. There, he restlessly paced the floor in awaiting the call from Timothea. He was now becoming annoyed with himself for having invited that weird woman to lunch. ("What on earth did I do that for? Things can't be as bad as she's saying. They can't be! It's an exaggeration.")

Increasingly, he felt that his happy mood had been forcibly changed by Anna. He had a sensation like that of a black cloud slowly coming up and turning the day's blue sky darker.

In addition to being annoyed with himself, he also annoyed Mrs Collop. He couldn't resist going downstairs, on the very verge of the evening meal, to knuckle her office window.

"Have there been any calls for me, Mrs Collop? Either this afternoon or this evening?"

"If there was," she frostily retorted, "I would have either notified you or put it through."

"Sorry," he hastily cried. "Sorree!"

The PBX buzzed loudly a fair number of times for the rest of the evening.

Not one buzz was for Peter.

II

The following day, Friday, had a sky as blue as the day before, but Peter's mood was now darkening it even more. He had to *make* himself walk to the nearby British Museum (his long-time familiar haunt); but he was unable to enjoy the refreshing company of the exhibits (especially the Egyptian) which had always been his routine. He was soon turning back, walking at an ever-increasing stride. Clashing within him were his worry about Rafe and the anxiety that he, Peter, might be missing a precious call from Timothea.

Also, he had the prospect of a lunch with that weird woman. Hanging over him like another dark cloud!

At lunch, Anna Yosenhants was not pleased to find that his eyebrows were continually being raised in expectation every single time Mrs Collop entered the restaurant. He even half-rose from his chair at an especially audible buzz from the PBX. Anna knew herself to be an exceptionally attractive woman. She was quite different, of course, from Timothea. She wasn't so pocket-sized and her hair was a gleaming blonde – unlike Timothea's hair which was fully and flowingly raven-dark. And Timothea's lips were of the lightest cherry. Anne's lips were orange. But, although

Ann had no designs upon a man old enough to be her father, it is understandable to us that she was a little miffed at not being the centre of a man's full attention, a man who was still physically eligible.

Re-adopting her classical-secretarial role, she paused over the famous rissole. She leaned forward.

"Mr Smith, is my presence no longer of any interest to you? Did you not hear my question?"

He displayed instant remorse. "I'm so sorry. I do beg your pardon. Would you very kindly repeat the question?"

"I was venturing to ask why your cottage is called Meadow Cottage. Does it have a meadow?"

"It does indeed. A lovely meandow. Not too large, but definitely a meadow. Full, at the moment, of buttercups and daisies and soon to fill still more with still more wild flowers."

"I have to say," said Ann, after a pause and dropping her frigid manner, "that I'm deeply impressed. What a blessing it must be at times of stress and strain!"

"There are six bee-hives at the far end."

"Six?" Ann was both moved and astounded. "You mean to say you keep bees?"

"Oh, no, I never handle them. I just simply let Mr Mullins use the meadow. They're his bees. He lives in another part of the hamlet. Hasn't got a meadow, you see, or even much of a garden."

"Is this, then, a business arrangement?"

"Not really, no. But I get a rake-off in the shape of the product – for my own use and to give to friends and so on. Honey from the meadow-bees."

"Oh, Peter," said Anna, all smiles, "what a lovely phrase! Honey from the meadow-bees."

"Would you sometimes like to have a pot?"

"Oh, yes please!"

The lunch progressed more favourably after this happier note. Peter had relaxed. He was still longingly hopeful, but his disappointment had become more bearable. Anne brightly said: "I gather that my boss has often visited the cottage?"

"Oh, yes. With Lizzie-Wizzie and the kiddie-winkies. When they were young. Not so much now."

Slightly revolted by the baby-language, Anna said: "We must make sure he continues to visit."

"He's always welcome. And Lizzie-Wizzie."

Ann decided to change tack slightly. "How far is the cottage from the village? From Poyton?"

"Oh, not that far. But, as I've mentioned, I'm in the hamlet. A bit further on. But that means, you see, that I get main drainage and electricity."

"I'm glad to hear that," said Anna, and she immediately regretted saying so. (Would Peter think she was angling for an invite? Or even to buy the place?) To her own alarm and dismay, she compounded the first of these risks. She said: "I've never been to that part of the country before."

She was given no time to mitigate these words (which did indeed cause Peter to give her a bit of a special glance). Mrs Collop had appeared in the doorway to the restaurant. She signalled at Peter.

He blushed. He jumped up. Anna felt able to laugh a little. "Why, Peter – you're blushing!"

"Please, just excuse me a moment," and he dashed out to Mrs Collop's office.

He did register that Mrs Collop was being a bit stiff and disapproving about something (he had not yet told her of his engagement), but he was too overjoyed to care. She shut him in with her managerial telephone. He launched into an ecstatic and instant salutation.

"Oh, Timothea, my lovely one! Tell me! Put me out of my misery! Is it the man from the Milk Marketing Board you wish to marry? Or is it I, the poverty-struck woodworker?"

We must bowdlerise the foul and obscene response which came snarling down the phone.

"What the bloody hell," said Peter's ex-wife, "are you bloody well playing at now?"

Peter went white over this form of shock and could hardly speak. He managed to say: "I thought you were someone else. Why have you phoned me?"

"Because you've had the bloody nerve to bloody well cancel the meeting with MY solicitor. You'll pay for this, I can tell you! So there's someone you is going to marry, is there? I get it. You reckons you is going to reduce my money! You bloody can't, you—"

And there followed a stream of abuse so cloacal that Peter too disgusted to do or say anything else other than to put down the phone.

Mrs Collop was watching him through the window to her indoor office. Her nose was pretty much stuck to the glass, and her eyes were full of even stiffer disapproval. Mr Peter Smith only then realised that his ex-wife had been doing her most recent best to defame him, and had succeeded. Coldly shivering, he joined Mrs Collop at the same time as Anna came out of the restaurant looking enquiringly concerned.

"That was my ex-wife," he told Anna. "You were right. She's obviously been telling lies about me even to Mrs Collop. I have to accept it. Even my long-time friendship with Mrs Collop has now been destroyed. Mrs Collop, I shall leave your hotel tonight and never return to it again. Please make up my bill."

The reaction to Peter's decision was a flood of tears and a promise never to believe a single word of what the ex-wife might have the evil audacity to phone and say again.

"Very well," said Peter, but he felt a bit guilty about Mrs Collop as he walked Anna back to Russell Square.

"She's always been decent to me," he said, "for many years. But I just had to tick her off. I couldn't have her repeating those sort of stories about me. But I must say I just can't understand all this. What on earth could have got into poor old Elsie? A harmlessly simple woman like that!"

Anna firmly said: "It's something you have to face, that's all. People change."

"But not as drastically as that, surely?"

"They do, Peter – they do! Face it."

Peter sighed as deeply as any disillusioned philosopher and said: "In future, I suppose, we'll have to refer to her as Madam Ex or something. Yes, Madam Ex. That, I think, will do. We'll only refer to her as Elsie if she returns to normal."

Anna said: "Let's find a bench and sit down."

"Shouldn't you be back at work," said Peter, instantly worried on her behalf. "I don't want you getting the sack."

"Peter, please don't worry your pretty little head," and she slipped her arm through his and took him to the secluded bench. They carefully sat down. She went on: "Friday afternoon is when we high and mighty ones take nearly all our work home to finish off. I live only just round the corner. I can easily make up for any work-time I spend on dilly-dallying with a Mr Peter Smith."

Peter was still looking very pale. He couldn't seem to find the strength to reply. He didn't even reply when she encouragingly said: "Is this, perhaps, the very bench where you and my boss used to eat your youthful sandwiches?"

Still no reply. Suddenly, he jerkily said: "She was never like that when we were married. She was just dull and, frankly, rather boring."

"Then why did you marry her? Was she so devastatingly attractive?"

"No, she wasn't. I don't like saying it, but she wasn't attractive at all. Not ugly, of course, but definitely not attractive. And she never used the kind of language I heard her use today. I couldn't possibly repeat it."

"Peter, I have already experienced her flow of foul language."

"I can only apologise for her and say how sorry I am that she's bothered you."

"Peter, don't be daft! Just tell me one thing. Why did you marry her? Was it blackmail?"

"Blackmail? Oh, dear me – not blackmail. I think it was because I wanted to please her parents."

"My God! To please her parents?"

"You see, they were very nice people."

"Oh, that's a very sensible reason!"

"No, really. They were very nice. I was very young and I was their lodger. In Hackney, where her father had a wood-work business. My private workshop at the cottage is modelled upon his."

"All this," said Anna, fighting down her growing impatience, "doesn't explain why you married this terrible woman."

"Well, you see, I was very much from their sort of background. Lower middle-class, I suppose it's called. Or perhaps even lower. But they were very proud when I somehow got engaged to their daughter. I went to a grammar-school, you see."

"Oh, that explains everything!"

"It does, actually. It gave me a lot of polish. I didn't do terribly well academically. But it did give me polish. Not too shiny, I hope. But polish."

"Polish? You mean social polish?"

"Yes, polish. I got even more polish out of National Service – in the Army."

"You were in the Army? Were you ever in a battle?"

"Oh, no," he said, rather drily, "the real war was over. I just missed the post-war battles which people now forget. Had I been in the Suffolks, perhaps, I could have got myself killed in Malaya – or in Korea with the Durhams But no. I was posted back to my own training battalion in Aldershot. Training a platoon."

"Are you telling me you were an officer?"

"Yes. And it gave me, as I say, even more polish. The Army was a bit snobbish in those days. Grammar-school boys were not regarded as quite as top-notch as other boys. But most of the chaps were very nice people. I had a good time, which included time to pop in and see how the old magazine was getting on. And, of course, to see Rafe upstairs. We were very young men."

Anna stood up. Peter, of course, instantly stood up too. She said: "Peter, I think I now understand you a little better, even if I still don't understand why you married that woman."

"I can only tell you that her parents were absolutely delighted when I called on them in my uniform. It was such a delight to see their faces."

"And how did Madam Ex react to your uniform?"

"Not with any great excitement. None at all, in fact. She didn't even seem to recognise me."

"What about your own parents?"

"Oh," he said, in a strangely off-hand way, "they had been killed towards the end of the War."

"Peter, I'm sorry."

"Oh, that's all right. It was in 1944, just after D-Day. I'd taken my brother for a walk. He was six and I was thirteen. We saw a flying-bomb come over. It landed behind the trees in an area where we lived. A big black cloud came up from behind the trees, very slowly. And when we got home, we found it had killed both our parents."

"Peter," said Ann, "I'm sorry. I feel I've intruded."

"That, of course, was long before I met the very nice parents of Madam Ex."

"And, of course, before you met my boss?" Anna said this because she didn't know what else to say. He simply nodded vaguely and she still didn't know what else to say. So she added: "You didn't come across him in the Army, did you?"

"Oh, no. Rafe couldn't get in. He's the same age as me, of course. He had what they call a heart-murmur. It's not all that serious, I'm told, but the Army was very fussy on that score. That's why he went to university while I was in Aldershot. But Rafe would have made a very good officer."

"Peter, I'm sure you're right. I think I'd better get home to finish off my work. How long will you be staying in London?"

Instead of replying at once, Peter puzzled Anna by looking

down at his feet and slowly pacing in a small circle. He was looking at his feet as if wondering what they were doing. Eventually he came to a stop. He looked Anna full in the face.

He very gravely said: "I was planning to leave on Saturday, but I now think I might well go on Sunday. Or possibly Monday."

Trying to be brightly reassuring in being satirical, Anna said: "That's very clear thinking."

He did not smile. He said: "I think I perhaps ought to look in on Snookie Wookie."

As we have noted earlier, Peter was not without guile in springing a surprise statement. Anna at once said, as she was intended to: "Who on earth is Snookie Wookie?"

"My little-boy brother," said Peter, now breaking into a smile. "He was a lovely little kid. Everyone loved Snookie Wookie. He's grown up now, of course. Forty three. Haven't seen him for ages."

"Then perhaps," said Anna, "it's time you did."

"You really think so?"

"Well, since he's your little brother …"

"You think, perhaps, that Madam Ex may have got at him? That she might have been telling him lies about me?"

"Well, yes. That certainly looks like being a possibility."

"In that case, Anna, I will go and see him tomorrow. Lives in Hampstead. I'm afraid I've been a bit remiss about Snookie Wookie. I might need to be very firm with him if he's been corrupted."

"Having seen how you dealt with Mrs Collop, I'm sure you'll be reasonably capable."

"You really think so? Oh, good! It's been a pleasure having lunch with you, Anna."

"Thank you very much indeed for inviting me. I really did enjoy the Golconda Rissole. But goodbye for now," and she turned, giving him a departure-wave, charming but decisive.

Yet she couldn't help being struck by a fresh thought. She

turned back. She calmly said: "By the way, where did you go after you lost your parents? Might I ask?"

"From then on," came the reply, "we stayed with our granny. In London, of course. My dad's mother."

"Oh," said Anna perkily, "would that be Granny Smith you called her?"

"Why, yes! That's what she was called. Granny Smith."

"In other words, the same as the apple?"

"Oh, yes – the apple," and he was laughing so delightedly that she kissed his cheek.

"There you are," she said, "you have the seal of approval from Miss Frozen Pants herself."

"So you know they call you that?"

"An old and boring joke, Peter. Goodbye again."

"Goodbye for now," he said, and he called after her: "I think it's possible that Timothea has phoned by now."

There was something of a plaintive note in this last remark of Peter's. Anna was touched by it. Over her shoulder, she called back: "I hope so!"

Back at the Golconda, he found that Timothea had still not telephoned. But he was no longer so anxious. He felt creamily content. After all, had not Timothea herself said: "It can sometimes be jolly difficult to make a discreet phone call."

Or something like that she had said. He could not remember her exact words. But he remembered more clearly someone in the Officers' Mess saying: "Always give a girl-friend room to manoeuvre."

CHAPTER FOUR

Another Part of the Heart

I

Finishing his breakfast the next day (Saturday), Peter was no longer fretting over Timothea's failure to phone. He didn't fully appreciate, we have to say, that the birth of the supporting friendship with Anna was a big boost to his better mood.

"Very nice brekker," he said to his breakfast-waitress, and he gave her a tip so generous that she gasped in astonishment.

By now, all the staff knew he was engaged to be married and had heard about the dreadful phone-call. Several of them were keen to shepherd him out of the hotel on his way to Hampstead. Smiles all round.

He had changed his jacket. Harris Tweed, he had decided, was a better garb for a place like Hampstead, as was the Harris Tweed cap which he wore in his cottage-garden at Poyton.

But he did not fully appreciate that he was foolishly vulnerable to his brother's tendency to cadge. Peter had, in fact, already written the cheque (stored in his wallet) for no less than five hundred pounds. He was looking forward to presenting it to poor little Snookie Wookie.

"I've neglected the poor little chap far too long," he actually muttered to himself on the tube-train.

We have to say that he seemed to have forgotten that a wonderful child can be a bit different from a man of forty-three. Peter still saw him as that child. He still saw him, too, as the sort of child he would love to have in a loving marriage. Yes, Peter was indeed day-dreaming of himself as a younger man married to Timothea. He was smiling as he thought of their first-born, a child as real to him, in his mind, as both the steam-train and the tube-train heading for Hampstead.

"Stand clear of the gates!"

Hampstead is still the deepest tube-station in London and the huge rising lift had come to a stop. Peter had heard those age-old recorded words many a time in visiting his brother, and, as he always did, he glowed with brotherly love.

He emerged from the street-level entry and jauntily made his way to a certain street which (for those days) had a "working-class" appearance and was therefore disreputable. The wrong sort of artists tended to live there.

Peter wasn't bothered by its reputation, but, as he made his way up the stairs to Snookie's flat above a poor-quality shop, he did worry about the amount of rubbish and real dirt in the passageway. It seemed to have got worse since his last visit. He feared for his brother's health and was beginning to frown.

Even the door looked grubby. He pressed the bell-push fastidiously, with his little finger.

Snookie opened the door boisterously. He was totally bald and looked older and less healthy than Peter.

"Welcome, old chap," he cried, copying Peter's known manner. (He was henceforth to struggle in keeping the sneer out of his voice.) "Long time no see, eh? Come in!"

The flat, referred to by Snookie as his studio, was small, and as dirty as the approach to it. Peter felt it safest to sit on the extreme edge of the food-stained sofa.

"I've never seen this place looking so bad," said Peter, becoming severe. (As we have seen, he was capable of issuing a reproof.) Squintingly, he could see through an open door into the untidy kitchen. Both the sink and the draining-board were piled with unwashed crockery and utensils of every kind. He therefore added: "Don't you think it would be a good idea occasionally to do the washing-up?"

"Oh," said Snookie, deliberately insolent, "Granny Smith can come in and do it."

"Granny Smith," Peter said, as patiently as if to a child, "is dead you see. So she can't."

"In that case, dear brother, some other old bag can come in and do it."

Snookie was being provocative but, even to his own surprise, he saw a smile slowly spreading all over Peter's face.

"Do you know," said Peter, "that I used to think of Granny Smith without realising, until yesterday, that it's the same name as the apple."

"The apple? What apple?"

"The Granny Smith apple."

"How very interesting," said Snookie, after a pause. "What's the matter with you today? You seem strange."

Still smiling: "Yes, I do feel strange, I admit to it. I suppose it's because I've got such happy news. Snookie, old chap, I am engaged to be married."

To Peter's obvious disappointment, his beloved brother, the brother he had led by the hand on many a childhood walk, showed not the slightest curiosity on hearing this news. He simply lit a cigarette and sat smoking it while staring at the mantelpiece.

In following Snookie's stare, Peter jumped to his feet. He strode to the mantelpiece, but did not touch the wedding-photograph which stood there. It was in black and white, and it showed Madam Ex in her wedding-dress and with Peter at her side. Peter was unable to speak for several moments, then chokingly, he said to Snookie: "What is this doing here? Did you put it here deliberately? To upset me?"

Snookie pretended to be agitated in the face of this abrupt accusation. Cunningly, he protested: "Honestly, I came across it and just thought it should go on show. After all, it's a family thing. I'm in it as well. I think I look quite good."

Peter slowly sank down on the sofa. "I'm sorry, old chap, for what I just said. It's not your fault, at all, but I've only just found out that her behaviour has been so evil-minded that she makes me feel quite sick. She phoned me up. It was terrible to hear her – horrible. I had no idea she was in any way that sort of person."

"Peter," said Snookie, "I'll get rid of it if that's what you want. I'm sorry. I'm shocked by what you've told me. I don't know what to say."

Peter stood up. "I think I'd like to go now. I'll be in touch. Meanwhile," and he took out his wallet and presented the cheque, "I hope this helps you out a bit."

"Oh, thank you! What a truly wonderful big brother I've got! You've saved my life again."

Peter said goodbye only in a series of quick little nods before hurrying off with his head down.

Snookie closed the door upon his brother's departure and stubbed out his cigarette.

He went to the door of his bedroom and opened it. He said: "He's gone now. You can come out. As usual, he didn't stay long. I told you, didn't I?"

We, the Olympian observers of these scenes, are quick to recognise the figure sitting quietly on Snookie's bed, her feet plonked heavily on the little bedside mat. She was the bride from the photograph, Madam Ex herself. She looked blankly disinclined to move or to speak.

Snookie advanced upon her. "Rouse yourself, you fat old lump!"

She was not as fat as the jubilantly spiteful Snookie was implying. She was simply big-boned and stocky. Also, she was not old although no longer young. She was actually two years younger than Peter, the man whose wife she had been.

She did now move, but slowly and only to turn her head and look Snookie full in the face. Just as slowly, she raised her arm – her very ample arm. Snookie backed away hastily. She had only raised her arm to enable herself to scratch the side of her neck. Snookie was not to know this, was he? He knew, as much as we would, that a blow from Madam Ex would be like a forearm-smash by an all-in wrestler. It would have sent him flying backwards across the room. Snookie was not all that brave a man, but he had his pride.

"Look here," he said, unwittingly copying the sometimes stern tones of his brother, "are you going to do the washing-up or are you not?"

Having finished her slow scratch, Madam Ex went out to the kitchen without a word and did as ordered. It was done at her own pace but efficiently and neatly. Snookie retired to the sofa and put his feet up. Another cigarette. He was very pleased with his morning's work.

"Elsie," he said, raising his voice while lazily inspecting his cheque, "did you manage to hear what my barmy brother was saying?"

"Wasn't lissnin," was her quiet reply, so quiet that Snookie assumed she was as deaf as ever.

It had long been unwise of him, as well for some others, to assume that she had a hearing problem. It was also unwise of him, in his particular case, to tell her a lie which she knew to be untrue. He got up from the sofa to tell her this lie while she finished the last of his dirty dishes.

From behind her and close into her ear, he said: "Peter hates you. He has always hated you. He told me again this morning."

She became suddenly motionless. She stared through the

kitchen window above the sink. All she could see was a red brick wall. She said, again in a low voice: "That aint what Peter wooder said when I addim."

Snookie didn't even bother to wait for (or hear) her reply. He was back on the sofa with his feet up. Within a few more moments, she was carefully draping the tea-towel in total completion of her task. She came into the sitting-room and sat down in the armchair opposite the sofa. Her hands were in her lap like two dead fish.

"Elsie," said Snookie, sitting up a little, "would you like me on the bed?"

"Not today, thank you," she placidly said.

He was not in the least offended. He lay back contentedly to say: "That's all right then. I'd get more fun on the bed with a sack of potatoes."

Madam Ex, too, didn't seem to be offended. This, we must conclude, is surely a most extraordinary relationship?

Let us examine it further.

Snookie demandingly said: "Well? Aren't you going to get going on the phone?"

"No I aint," said Elsie, not defiantly but as a dull statement of fact. She seemed to be sinking even more deeply into the armchair and becoming as immovable as a huge boulder of clay.

Snookie leapt up from off the sofa. He almost screamed: "Then why the bloody hell have you come over? What are you doing here?"

"I just fort," she said, in the same dull voice, "that you might want sunnick done like the washing-up."

"Elsie, you are mucking up my plan. Why are you mucking up my plan?"

"I dunno, Snookie. I dunno what you mean."

"But you've been a good girl up till now! What's the matter with you?"

"I dunno. I just aint in the mood."

Snookie was getting angry. "Who cares what mood you're in?

Just do as you're told and everything will be all right. We need to do more on the phone."

"I doesn't wanna go on the blower no more," said Elsie. "I doesn't like saying them fings you learn me to say."

Snookie was outraged. "Me? I don't tell you what to say! It all comes from you, Elsie – from deep down in your mind. Everything you've been saying is of your own free will. Every filthy dirty little thing."

He suddenly began to wheedle. "Now come along, Elsie. I'll dial the number as I always do. All you have to do is to say what you want to say. Be a good girl and I'll go on being nice to you. You need to speak to Miss Box at the Institute."

Dull stubbornness from Elsie: "I doesn't wanna ring the hinstitute."

"I'm not asking you to ring the Institute. It's Saturday today. The Institute is shut. Miss Box is AT HOME! That's where we ring her. You need to warn her about the man she's working for."

"What man would that be, Snookie?"

"Don't call me Snookie! How many more times do I have to tell you?"

"All right, Snookie. I'll try me best. But oo's this man you is talkin abart?"

Even Snookie was now getting confused. "What man?"

"The man you say we has to ring up. Would that be my Peter that was?"

"Not him," screamed Snookie. "It's Miss Box we've got to phone! Miss Box, his secretary at the Institute!"

"So we does phone the hinstitute?"

Snookie went over to the phone, which was on the sideboard, and began dialling. His whole face was tight with fury and malice.

"All you have to do," he said, covering the mouthpiece as the distant-end rang, "is to warn her, as a friend, that she working for a naughty man. A nasty man. A man with a dirty filthy mind."

"I'm sorry, Snookie, but I'm not in the mood to do this – not this time. I dunno really why I said the things I said to Peter when I runged him afore. I doesn't want to ring Peter agin."

Snookie slammed the phone down. "It's bloody Miss Box we need to ring! But what does it matter? You've sabotaged my whole plan. I can't go on."

"What plan is that, Snookie?"

"Never you mind," he said, barely able to control himself. "You're incapable of understanding it." He flung himself on the sofa, petulantly. "I honestly don't know what my brother ever saw in you. It's a mystery. How was he able to see your great fat arse, every day, without wanting to kick it black and blue?"

"I dunno, Snookie. I real don't."

But Snookie, at this point, suddenly became inspired. He calmed down. He rose from the sofa, smiling in satisfaction at his own cleverness.

"Why Elsie," he said, almost affectionately, "I think you're right! We don't need to phone Miss Box. All we need to do is to scare Peter into thinking you might phone her."

Madam Ex humbly asked: "Is this a change of plan?"

"No, Elsie. It's just a change of tactics. You won't need to do any more phoning. You've done enough to scare him. And I'll be scaring him still more when I next see him. What's the name of that woman he wants to marry? Have you remembered it yet?"

"What woman, Snookie?"

The woman he mentioned," said Snookie, beginning to speak through clenched teeth, "when you phoned him at that bloody awful hotel."

"I'm sorry, Snookie. I just can't member it."

"Not to worry," he generously said. "I'll soon winkle it out of him and where she lives. He'll soon be confiding in me because I'm his loving brother. And I'll make him really afraid you'll phone her. And then, see, I'll advise him to buy you off with the biggest sum of money we've ever got out of him! Get it?"

"Not really, no. I just don't want to do no more phoning up."

"Listen, Elsie. Let's put it like this. Just keep your stupid mouth shut and don't give the game away."

"Keep my stupid mouth shut," repeated Madam Ex, as obediently as if she were in Sunday school. "But there's one thing I doesn't get at all. Why do you keep talking about Pete as if he wore a naughty man? A nasty man? He wore never like that when I addim, not never. E didn't like me avin the telly on all day and things like that, but e wore never nasty about it."

"My God, Elsie," cried poor old Snookie, "you really are impossible. Have you clean forgotten what he was like when he took us off to bloody Southwold? Walking up and down along past the beach and looking at all the girls! Watching them undress! Time and time agin, hoping to see what he could see when they were undressing."

Madam Ex simply said: "I never did like that place. Sort of boring, I thought."

"You can say that again," said Snookie, and, to his annoyance she took him literally and said it again chantingly. "Sort of boring, sort of boring."

"Oh, get out and get back to Hackney," he said, pulling open his front door. "And bloody take that cheap and nasty handbag with you! Don't leave it behind."

Madam Ex obediently picked up the offending object and placidly said: "I dunno why you calls it cheap and nasty. You is the one oo gived it me."

"Only because," he yelled, "it's what suits you exactly! Now get out! OUT!"

Madam Ex annoyed Snookie still more by pausing to say: "And what does them other words mean?"

Almost a scream: "What other words?"

"Them words you learns me to say to nice Mister Rafe. E wore always nice to me. I don't wanna do them no more."

"Just get out of my sight," moaned poor Snookie, and he almost collapsed after shutting out Madam Ex.

II

Returning to that awful hotel in Bloomsbury (to use Snookie's description,) Peter was looking very worried indeed.

That wedding-photo on the mantelpiece had really shaken him up. To soothe himself, he had taken a very pleasant lunch in a small and overcrowded Hampstead restaurant (vegetarian, of course) and he had also gone for a long afternoon walk on Hampstead Heath. He did not, however, go to the National Gallery to look at Corot's lovely little picture entitled *The Bent Tree*. Peter and always gone to look at this picture every time he went to London. The fact that Peter had not was a major symptom of his disquieted soul. He spent the evening, after his late tea, in his somewhat austere room and in the broodingly uncomfortable arm-chair.

He found some solace in gazing at the telephone extension.

Would Timothea ring or wouldn't she?

She did not. By nine o'clock in the evening, he decided to ring Anna Yosenhants.

"Anna," he anxiously said, "I do hope this isn't an inconvenient time, but I've done something terrible. I need to talk to you about it."

"Something terrible? My dear new friend, what are you referring to?"

Thinking of the possibly eavesdropping Mrs Collop, all agog in her headphones at the PBX, he said: "It's not something I can discuss over the phone."

"And it's something terrible, you say?"

"Well, yes, I rather think so."

"You haven't gone and murdered Mrs Collop, have you?"

Mrs Collop was indeed listening and was not too pleased, but she did soften on hearing Peter hastily say: "Mrs Collop is a very dear friend of mine, Anna, may I ask you out to lunch again? Tomorrow? Sunday?"

In a cautious tone: "At the Golconda?"

"You can manage it, can't you? I do hope so."

"Tell me, Peter. Has Timothea rung you?"

"Not yet, no. Well? Can you come over? May I call and escort you here?"

After a slightly indrawn breath: "Peter, I think it would be better if you come over to my flat. It's only a stone's throw away," and, noting his hesitation, she added: "I promise faithfully that I won't try to seduce you."

"Anna," said Peter, rather sharply, "I only hesitated because I'm still hoping Timothea might call. Please take this matter seriously."

Anna quickly said: "Of course I'll take what ever you say very seriously. Look, let me make lunch for us. Spaghetti? Would that be all right? Grated cheese on top?"

"Thank you, Anna. Spaghetti, though. Would you mind very much breaking it into little bits before you cook it? I don't care for it in those long wormy-like strings. Ugh!"

A pause, then: "Why can't you cut it up for yourself after it's been served?"

"That, Anna, tends to be a bit messy. You might be interested to hear that Her Majesty the Queen is also of my opinion."

"When did you last have lunch with her?"

"Oh, I pop into Windsor every now and again," said Peter, his lightness of heart returning. "What time are *you* willing to grant me an audience?"

Anna laughed a little and said: "Peter, what time would be convenient for you?"

"I'm planning to go back home on the early-evening train from Paddington. So perhaps we should say twelve o'clock?"

"Come at eleven sharp," she assertively said, and she rang off without another word.

On Sunday and after a breakfast so slight as to be no real breakfast at all, Peter spent a lot of time in packing his suitcase. This, we can tell, was because he was still hoping for that phone-call. He had decided to pack his well-cut jacket but, as he had done on Saturday, to wear the trousers to it but with the Harris tweed jacket. A tweed cap, of course, is much easier to pack than a fetching trilby, so he decided to wear the fetching trilby for the visit to Anna's flat and for going home.

A lot was on his mind as he went down the stairs (with suitcase and raincoat) to pay off the old Mrs Collop. It was half-past ten and he was muttering about the train from Woodley Norton.

"What on earth can be wrong with Rafe? Why did he say what he said? The train did run and it very much a chuff-chuff!"

Mrs Collop said: "Pardon, Peter? What was that?"

"Nothing at all, Mrs Collop. I think I might be going slightly mad, that's all. It only remains for me to thank you for all the kindness you've shown me, and, of course, for the recipe."

To his embarrassment, Mrs Collop burst into tears. He hurried from the hotel as fast as he decently could.

He sat in Russell Square for a little while (Anna's flat was, as she had said, only a stone's throw away). He wanted to be exactly on time and had already found out the flat's exact location. But he was still worrying about Rafe in addition to his other worries.

When he came to be thumbing the bell-push to Anna's front door (in her massively splendid block), he was amazed at having the door flung open in that very second. His arm was seized and he was literally pulled inside.

Anna was being mischievously dramatic. "Tell me what you've done, old boy! Tell me all! What terrible thing has Peter Smith gone and done?"

Peter put down his suitcase and glanced nervously around. Anna's flat was of the impressively modern sort we would expect of a high-flying secretary. It prompted him into straightening his tie.

He said: "I don't really supose it's all that terrible in a physical sense. It's more the state of mind I'm in after having made a false assumption."

Anna put her hands on her hips in the manner of a stage-washerwoman. "Do you mean to tell me that I've been worrying all night about nothing? I thought you must have forged a cheque or something."

"Oh, it's nothing like that. But I did in fact write a cheque which I feel I shouldn't have done."

"And you don't have the funds to meet it?"

"Oh, nothing like that. I'm not a rich man. I'm often hard-pressed at times. I wouldn't write a cheque I couldn't cover. It was for five-hundred pounds, you see. For my son."

"Your son, you say?"

Peter hurriedly corrected himself. "My young brother, I mean. Why did I call him my son? Slip of the tongue, I suppose. But he really was a lovely little chap and I felt so sorry for him."

"Five hundred quid," said Anna, smoothly seating herself, "is quite a lot money even in this modern age. But what's so terrible about that if it's for someone you love?"

"That's the point, Anna. I don't think he deserved it. I think, in fact, that he's a bit of a shower."

Unfamiliar with Army slang, Anna said: "A what?"

"A bad chap – a rotter. It's too horrible to think about."

"When did you experience this earth-shaking revelation?"

"Almost as soon as I left his rather sordid little flat in Hampstead. He calls himself an artist, you see. But there's very little evidence that he actually does much work as an artist. He talks a lot about art, of course. Perhaps he has what is called a psychological block about what he wants to do. But I don't know. I think he might just be a rotter and not much more."

"Peter," Anna said, after a pause, "I think I'd better start the spaghetti. You'd better come and watch. See if I get things right."

She did not get things right in her gleamingly well-appointed kitchen. Although she concentrated hard, as he could see from her expression, she was feeding the spaghetti into the boiling water without first breaking it into little bits. Peter stood and gloomily watched, saying nothing in reproach. Essentially, he was a peace-loving man and always preferred to avoid extra controversy in times of discussion.

"Tell me," said Anna, when they sat down to the spaghetti. "Why exactly have you brought this matter of your brother to my attention? Was it actually important enough to make me worry all night?" (She was, of course, satirically exaggerating.)

"I'm so sorry you worried all night," said Peter, looking unhappily at the dish before him, "but may I have a small sharp knife please?"

All she had provided was a fork and a spoon, as she was quick to realise – along with her main and more serious omission.

"Oh, my God!" she cried, and she jumped up to fetch him the knife (and one for herself).

As Peter had mentioned, to cut up the spaghetti after it had been so well-presented turned it into quite a mess. The sauce and the curly cheese-shavings on top had all their tasty appearance destroyed.

"Peter," she felt obliged to confess, "I think I should tell you something. I am not a vegetarian. I love eating meat. I can't go without my daily meat. In fact, unthinkingly, I very nearly put a meat sauce into this concoction."

"I'm glad you didn't," was all Peter had to say on this, and very mildly.

After an innocuous dessert and during the well-approved-of coffee, Anna ventured to say: "Peter, it wasn't just you I was worrying about all night. It was my boss. He rang me from Brussels. He's become quite obsessed about this train-journey of yours."

Peter sighed in his perplexity. "I can't think why it so upsets him."

"He's also upset about the lady you met and decided to marry without even knowing if she's a vegetarian or not. He's not a vegetarian, as you must know, but he does know himself how important this will be to someone like you."

"It's so very kind of Rafe to be concerned," Peter said, again with a perplexed sigh. "But I do get on with meat-eaters fairly well."

"Nevertheless, Peter," said Anna, sharply, "it's a matter that bothers him on your behalf. Also, of course, the fact that he had asked me to make enquiries about your train."

"Oh, the train …"

"Yes, Peter – the train. I have checked. Peter, there was no steam-train on that line on Thursday. Furthermore, it wouldn't have been allowed. So what do you say to that?"

There were times in Peter's life when he could be stubborn. This was one of them. He said, politely but firmly: "Anna, I am not here to talk about the train or the woman I am going to marry."

Anna lost her temper slightly. "Then what are you here for?"

"I thought I'd made it plain. I'm here to talk about Snookie Wookie."

"For heaven's sake, Peter! That train and that mysterious woman you met – yes, my boss told me everything you told him – are more important than Snookie Wookie. You have to face reality."

"But I am facing reality."

"You're not!"

"Yes I am. I'm facing reality in the shape of Snookie Wookie."

Anna sat down on her impressive sofa to say: "All right, Peter. We'll put the matter of your friend's sanity and your sanity – and even my own sanity I am beginning to think – to one side. Let's give priority to the wretched Snookie Wookie."

Peter was in real distress here and Anna was well aware of that. He jumped up and began walking about the room while washing his hands with invisible soap and water – always a sign, in him, of a deep emotional crisis.

"At least," he said, in one of his sharper tones, "you've hit the nail on the head. Wretched is indeed the best way to describe my brother. It's almost too terrible to describe."

He was unable to speak for a few moments, so Anna said, in

his own sharp tone: "What exactly have you discovered, Peter? Tell me!"

Shivering all over as if he were inside a fridge, Peter sat down again to say: "You see, I didn't know I was wrong. The terrible thing is that I was wrong. It isn't Elsie who is controlling my brother. It's the other way round. It's Snookie himself who is controlling Elsie."

A pause. Anna coolly said: "Is Madam Ex no longer to be described as Madam Ex?"

"Her name is Elsie," snapped Peter. "And, as I say, it's Snookie who has her under his thumb."

Anna softened a little. "Peter. I'm sorry to hear this. But might I just ask how you came to change a conclusion we had both decided upon?"

"He gave himself away," said Peter, shivering with even greater intensity, "almost as soon as he let me into the flat. I told him, you see, that I was going to be married. I had thought he would be happy to hear that. But no, he didn't react at all. It sort of flashed into my mind that he already knew about Timothea."

"But Peter, how was that possible?"

Peter began to blush, which caused Anna to smile delightedly. "Peter, this is the second time I've seen you blush! Blushing like a village maiden – a man of fifty old enough to be my father! Oh, how wonderful!"

Peter spoke coldly and the blush began to ebb away. "If you must know, Miss Yosenhants, my assumption was based upon that phone-call which I received at the Golconda. Foolishly, I admit, I rushed to the phone thinking it was Timothea who had called. I didn't realise it was Elsie. I addressed her as Timothea, you see, I won't tell you what I said, but it was a most embarrassing thing to have done."

"In other words," said Anna briskly, "you had let the cat out of the bag."

"Well, yes – that's one way of putting it. But the point," said Peter who was still a bit uptight, "is surely obvious. It had to be Elsie who had told Snookie."

"About the cat?"

"What cat?"

"The cat, Peter, that you had let out of the bag – namely, that you had fallen for Timothea!"

"Well, yes – that just about sums it up. But there's more to it than met the eye," and here Peter's voice began to tremble. "Snookie had put an old photograph on the mantelpiece. It wasn't in a frame, just the photograph in a plain mount and propped up. The photograph of the wedding-group outside the church. My ghastly wedding. Ugh!"

Anna had become deeply thoughtful. She said: "And what did you make of that?"

"It was an act of spite. He was taunting me. He knows how unhappy the marriage was."

"Peter, could it perhaps have been a joke? A feeble joke, yes. But just a joke? Wedding-group photographs can be quite a hoot."

"I did think that myself, at first. But, after I had left the flat – which I did pretty quickly – I realised it had been done out of spite."

"Spite over what?"

"I don't yet know. I don't think I want to know."

"And yet you didn't think of stopping the cheque?"

"Of course not," said Peter, getting snappy again.

"Why not?"

"Because he's my brother."

"And you still love your brother?"

"Of course I still love him. He's my brother!"

Anna now surprised Peter more than she had ever done up till now. She got up and bolt-locked her advanced-security front-door.

Standing in front of him she said: "Peter I have now kidnapped you. I will not let you out and you will not catch your train this evening unless you answer the following question. Why did you marry Elsie?"

"I've already told you."

"You have not. I want a clear explanation that actually makes sense. As Miss Burgess used to say, let me make myself clear – "

Peter irritably interrupted. "What are you talking about? Who is Miss Burgess?"

"My old headmistress. A highly influential lady."

Peter jumped up to say: "Now look here, Anna. I haven't come here to play silly buggers."

In even more vigorous irritation, Anna said: "And I'm not here to allow two grown men, both old enough to be my father, to behave like idiots."

"Anna," said Peter in his severest tone, "may I ask how old you are?"

"Twenty-six, rising twenty-seven."

"As a mere twenty-six-year old, do you really think you're entitled to incarcerate a man old enough to be your father?"

"Yes, you silly old fool, I do."

"And do you, as a mere twenty-six-year old, accept that your definition of Elsie as evil could be quite wrong?"

"I'm willing to be convinced if you can convince me. But I've heard her voice. I've heard the foul flow of her language."

"I do remind you, Anna, that I've heard it too – and, in my surely valid opinion, I now believe she was not being her true self."

"Tell me, Peter. Is Elsie sleeping with your much-loved brother?"

"That's a most indelicate question. Why do you ask it?"

"Because, if she's the victim you claim her to be, then she would have to be under your brother's thumb totally. And totally means just that – soul and body. Oh, yes my boy! She's been having it off!"

"How can you possibly know that for certain?"

"Because intuition tells me that your brother is probably another example of an ambitious weakling. They often have a talent for manipulating their women."

"Oh dear," groaned Peter. "You're probably right."

"And I have another little bit of intuition to put before you. Was that money you gave your much-loved brother your holiday-money?"

Evasively, Peter said: "Well … not really."

"Was it or wasn't it? Or are you going to lie to me? As a friend? Lie to me? Eh? Well?"

"It was yes – the remainder of my holiday money. But it doesn't matter. I'm quite happy to go home a wee bit earlier than I had planned."

"There you are, you see," cried Anna, "another typical male idiot! Almost an exact copy of my boss."

"No, really," Peter tried to explain, "I'm happy to go home earlier because I want to make a special engagement-present for Timothea. It's a very nice Sheraton-style writing-desk which I'm restoring in my garden workshop. It has a really lovely little drawer, you know the sort? The sort that emits a little puff of air when you push it shut. So well-made, you see."

"Peter," said Anna, as sternly as she could, "you are attempting to throw sawdust in my eyes."

"I'm doing no such thing. I do really want to get back and finish restoring that desk."

"You will stay here, incarcerated, until you answer my question. Why did you marry that foul-mouthed female?"

Peter began his explanation jauntily and, one might say, recklessly. Sprawling back on the sofa, legs crossed and one arm extended nonchalantly, he said: "It's all because of the Old Kent Road really. Snookie and I were living with Granny Smith in New Cross, which, as you must know, is south of the river. The Thames. Old Father Thames."

"I don't know New Cross," said Anna. "Stick to the point."

"I am sticking to the point. I was seventeen and I was working in Russell Square at the magazine. My salary was two pounds a week. Can a youngster like you imagine what that meant?"

"It does seem low sum, even for those prehistoric days. But, as I say, stick to the point."

"The point, madam, is that I was too hard up to afford the train-fare on the crowded commuter trains. I had to cycle all the way up the Old Kent Road."

"To Russell Square, you mean?"

"Exactly. You're now getting the point, I hope. The Old Kent Road, and then having to cycle over London Bridge – especially in bad weather – was spoiling my life. So it was decided, in consultation with our Granny, that I should find lodgings north of the river. Which I did. I found lodgings in Hackney with the very nice parents of a young woman, then aged fifteen and named Elsie."

"Peter, I am now getting the point. But don't turn it into a prevarication. I'm warning you."

"Be patient with me, Anna, I beg of you," and Peter's tone was suddenly no longer so easy-going. He sat up more rigidly to add: "It was easier to cycle from Hackney to Russell Square. I never really noticed Elsie, not to begin with. She was so quiet and, although rather stocky, not very noticeable at all."

Anna said: "This was in the early stages of post-war recovery, was it?"

"If you could call it recovery, yes. People were still very hard up. That's why Elsie's parents were grateful for my ten bob a week rent. Elsie herself had to go out to work, but I didn't know where. I simply wasn't interested. I often went back to see Granny and Snookie, of course, but that was at week-ends. Then, one day, when it was raining and not very pleasant, I did notice Elsie. It was on a Saturday when I didn't go back to New Cross. Because it was such a nasty day, you see."

Peter's voice cracked a little as he said this, and Anna began to look at him very carefully.

"She was working, as it turned out, for a not very nice stall-holder in the market. He sold vegetables which were always heaped on the stall under a sort of tarpaulin roof."

Peter's voice was really breaking up now. He went on: "I was walking past this stall, I saw Elsie standing beside this stall. She wasn't quite underneath the tarpaulin roof. She had been left alone there, presumably in charge of the stall."

Anna asked: "What was she selling?"

"Parsnips," said Peter, "but she was not selling them very successfully. They were wet, they were covered in soil, they were untrimmed and the entire stall was heaped with them. Heaped!"

Peter couldn't seem to speak for a few moments until Anna said, quietly: "Go on."

He said: She was standing there and she was holding out two of these parsnips in one of her hands. Her sleeves were wet and she was wearing a sack around her waist. Not a proper apron. Just a sack. She looked at me. I looked at her. She said nothing. I said nothing. I simply walked on."

He stopped speaking. He was obviously in distress over this memory, but it was a puzzled form of distress. He was unable, it seemed, to understand himself. He was not upset to the point of tears, but he was looking deeply moved.

"I was so sorry for her," he at last said. "I was so filled with pity. I don't know how it all happened, but I began taking her to the pictures and even to a terrible dancing-hall at one time. I honestly don't know why I asked her to marry me. It was pity. I married her out of pity."

Anna quietly said: "No, Peter. It wasn't pity. It was love."

"How on earth," he said, "can you possibly say that? You're so wrong. It was pity."

"No," she said more sharply, "it was love, you idiot. I know all about pity. I once worked for a charity in my more idealistic youth. A lot of people donated money out of pity – a very dubious state of mind. It's a main component is fear and sometimes moral vanity. Some did donate out of love. Not many."

"But Anna," said Peter, "she was so pathetic. It just broke my heart to see her trying to sell those dirty old parsnips. And a sack for an apron."

"And I say again, Peter. It was love you felt – not pity. You went a bit too far, I would say, in offering to marry her. But the fact remains. It was love you felt. It's different from the love you feel for Timothea It was love of a different sort from another part of the heart. But it was love. It's often known quite simply as being kind. Surely you're old enough to know that? You, Peter, are an idiot. No other word for it."

Anna got up and unbolted the door with no further ado.

Peter emitted a long sigh of recovery and said; "I suppose you're right. I am an idiot."

"We're all idiotic at various times," said Anna. "Help me to do the washing-up."

After this small ritual was completed, Anna led the way back into the lounge and said: "Might I just ask you something intimate? What did Elsie say when you proposed marriage?"

"Oh," said Peter, more-or-less himself again, "she simply said: all right."

"Just those words?"

"Yes. Elsie, you must understand, was not too great at making conversation."

"Are you saying she's stupid?"

"I am not. People make a bad mistake if they think her stupid. She passed her driving-test, for instance, the very first time she took it. I, on the other hand, had to take the test three times."

"So did I," murmured Anna, and again looked very thoughtful. After a few more moments, she said: "Might I also just ask something more? What did Elsie actually say when you suggested divorce?"

"She said the same words again: all right."

"So she never caused you any real trouble?"

"Not her personally, no. It was that solicitor of hers. A nasty piece of work. It's beginning to dawn on me that very possibly Snookie Wookie is somehow in cahoots with him."

Anna and Peter were now pleasantly re-seated in the lounge. Anna said: "I shall be giving some thought to this brother of yours."

Peter instantly said: "Would you like to see a photograph of him? When he was a little boy?"

"Why, yes. Do you have one with you?"

"I do indeed. I have it in my wallet," and Peter produced the photograph, a snapshot but one that bowled Anna over immediately.

"By God, what a lovely little boy! Oh, it's making me go all broody! What a charmer! Put it away. It could ruin all my plans."

"Most people," said Peter, a shade proudly, "say much the same," but he replaced it in his wallet sadly. "It's terrible to think of him turning out so badly."

"How did he come to be living in Hampstead?"

"Because Granny Smith left him the house in New Cross. He inherited it when he was eighteen. He had to do his National Service, of course, and he didn't like that. He resented the fact that he wasn't given a commission. He went off the rails a bit when he was discharged. Against all advice, including mine, he sold the house and bought a grotty flat in Hampstead. He wanted to be among what he called the artistic fraternity."

This was quite a long explanation by Peter, but it interested Anna. She said: "I know something about property-values. He's possibly smarter than you think. Property in Hampstead will be fabulous in price within a few years, even for grotty flats."

"That may be so," Peter said heavily, "but it will be the bank who will benefit. He's in debt up to his neck and even beyond."

"Oh, dear! Then perhaps he's not so smart."

"Oh, I think we can call him smart," and Peter sounded a shade bitter here. Anna mistook this tone and quickly said: "Wasn't this legacy a bit unfair on you?"

"Not at all," was the reply that surprised her. "It was an agreed arrangement. I inherited the property of our other granny –

Granny Pringle. Our two grannies were very friendly with each other."

"Not always a common occurrence."

"I've heard that said. But, in our case, our two grannies were lovely. Snookie and I, in fact, were allowed to evacuate to Oxfordshire – to Granny Pringle's cottage – during the war. Snookie didn't like it there. He's not a country boy. As soon as it was safe, we had to come back to New Cross. Back to Granny Smith."

"To please Snookie?"

"That's correct. To please Snookie."

"And when did you actually inherit this very nice cottage of yours?"

"Two years after I married Elsie."

"And how did she like it there?"

"Elsie didn't like it at all. She wasn't unpleasant about it, but she, like Snookie, is a Londoner born and bred. She pined for Hackney. Pined."

"Even so," said Anna, who was genuinely ignorant of the preferences of the lower classes, "I can't understand why anyone wouldn't like a nice little country cottage."

"What you don't understand, Anna, is that it was not a nice little country cottage. Have you any idea of what the real country was like at that time?"

Peter's tone was getting a bit sharp again. Anna amicably said: "Well I am only a sentimental townee myself. I'm helplessly romantic about the country."

"Even in Oxfordshire," Peter quite snappily said, "villages could be as slummy as anything you find in the East End of London. More so, I'd say. I can remember my mother telling me about it. She was brought up without main drainage and without mains water. Even when Snookie and I were there during the war, it was an earth-coset in the garden and a well for the entire hamlet – just one well, often with dead rats being fished up out of it."

Anna hastily said: "All right, Peter. Please don't shatter all my illusions."

She had stood up and had drifted over to the big window in the lounge. She immediately said: "Peter, come here! Quickly! Look at the street!"

He joined her at the window. He looked down at the street below (this was a high flat) and it seemed to be empty of people and traffic. Usually and obviously, it was a busy street, but now it seemed to be in the throes of a sudden lull.

It only lasted for a second or two. Anna had put her hand to his face to turn it towards hers, saying: "Look at me, Peter," and he did so.

"Now look back at the street," she said, and it was just as suddenly full of traffic in what had to be its normal way.

"That's quite extraordinary," he said.

"Yes," she said, as they both returned to the sofa. "And I daresay there's a rational explanation. It's not something that everyone perceives. But I have seen it happen just once in Russell Square when I glanced out of our office window. A sudden lull. The whole square suddenly devoid of human activity."

"Most extraordinary," was all Peter could find to say about it.

"Peter," she said, "is that what happened?"

"Anna," he diffidently said, "I don't know what you mean. We both saw what happened. We know it happened . A bit strange, but, as you've said, there's probably an explanation."

"Yes, Peter. But did anything like that happen to you on Thursday? The day you came to London?"

Peter suddenly remembered. "Well yes," and he laughed slightly. "Now you've mentioned it, the same thing happened to me on Woodley Norton station."

"There was one of these sudden lulls?"

"That's right – it was very much the same sort of thing. The whole station seemed devoid of all human activity, apart from one oldish porter – and not very well-mannered – and me and just the chap in the ticket-office. And even he, like the porter, seemed totally unfamiliar. Perhaps I had seen them before. I don't know. But the train came in and I had to scramble aboard before I had any time to be anything other than rather annoyed."

"And shortly after that experience, you met up with the love of your life?"

"In one of the empty first-class compartments, yes. Most extraordinary, I suppose, when one thinks about it in a cold and logical sort of way."

"So you can see why my boss is both baffled and worried by your account of it all?"

"I certainly can't blame him for finding it all a bit hard to believe. But it did happen."

"And I believe you, Peter. I believe in your train. I believe it was a steam-strain and it did run. I'm old enough, you know, to remember steam-trains myself! I travelled to and from to my awful boarding-school on such a train. We all had our hockey sticks with us."

"That's something else that puzzles me," said Peter, genuinely puzzled about it. "Why do girls going off to their boarding-schools – or coming back from them – always carry their hockey-sticks? Am I being obtuse here? Is there a rational explanation?"

"Of course there is," said Anna, in sudden asperity, "if you bother to think!"

Peter obligingly started to think about this conundrum and began saying: "I suppose, if one thinks about a male item of sport – such as a cricket-bat – we can perhaps work out that – "

Anna interrupted with affectionate impatience but real impatience nonetheless. "Oh, for heaven's sake don't start rambling off about our hockey-sticks! Can't you see the importance of this discussion? We, both of us, have experienced this strange lull in activity that seems to happen from time to time – and always unexpectedly. Weird. What do you think it means?"

Peter thought for a few moments and then carefully said: "It could mean, I suppose, that it could be due to some sort of mental blackout."

Anna almost shrieked: "Oh, what an idiot! How can two people have such a mental blackout at the exactly the same time?"

"Anna, I do see what you mean. I definitely do see. Incidentally, I have sometimes noticed that this lull in activity sometimes happens out in the countryside. The leaves can seem to stop moving. The birds, too, can seem to stop twittering. Even the rabbits can suddenly stop and look as if they're made of stone. All very odd. Only for a second or so. Perhaps less. It's not something I've noticed very often."

"Well, Peter, the lull we saw in the street below these flats was at least two seconds. I've never actually seen it from these windows before."

"And you saw it from the windows of your office in Russell Square. I can only say that I never witnessed any such lull when I used to work in that same building."

"That, Peter, doesn't mean it never happened. It simply means you never noticed. But can't you see what I'm trying to tell you?"

"I must admit, Anna, that I don't quite see what you're worrying about."

"I'm worrying about the fact that my boss and your special friend thinks you're mad. I can't say it too forcibly. Insane was the word he used."

"Oh, dear," said Peter. "That's putting it a bit too forcibly, I'd say. All the same, he'll have to change his mind – won't he? – when he meets Timothea. She'll be back in Stratford in just seven days. I think I'm right. I'm sure she said so."

"Peter, he actually believe that's she's a delusion of yours – that she doesn't exist."

"How utterly ridiculous!"

"I agree. And, as I've already tried to emphasise, I believe in your steam train. It was magical, yes. But magic does happen in real life. You have my full support."

"Thank you very much, Anna," he said, with genuine warmth and friendliness.

"I don't want to see you two utter chumps falling out over this. That's why I'm so relieved to have proved to you that you didn't have a mental blackout. He's got a very good argument. You might find yourself beginning to believe him."

Peter laughed heartily. "Oh, that will never happen! I think I'd better go now," and he looked at his watch. "I reckon I could catch an earlier train – only because," he hastened to add, "I really do want to finish restoring that desk. It really is a very nice desk."

"I look forward to seeing it, Peter."

"Oh, you will! You will! Thanks for the spaghetti," and he picked up his suitcase and coat.

At that very moment when Anna was about to open the front door, there came a ring at the bell.

She opened the door. A bashful but chunkily handsome man was revealed. He was carrying an expensive box of chocolates in one hand and a smallish suitcase in the other.

"Here I am," he said. "Dead on time!"

Anna was not in the least embarrassed by this development. She simply groaned and said: "Oh, no Felix. I'm sorry. I'm not in the vein. Go and see Midge. She would love to see you, I'm sure."

"But Anna," this fellow wailed. "You promised me!"

"I know, Felix, but I am not in the vein. Do as you're told. I'll phone Midge and tell her you're on your way," and, to Peter, she said: "Goodbye for now, Peter," and shut the door on both the two men.

They both stood waiting for the lift to rise from the depths. The Felix chap looked at Peter's far bigger suitcase and said: "How long has she let you stay?"

Although somewhat naïve, Peter was no greenhorn. He was also a tolerant man. He simply said: "Not long," and said no more until he was in the street and had hailed a good old London taxi-cab.

"Paddington Station, please."

His only interest, for the time being, was in finding out why Rafe was so upset about the chuff-chuff.

On the concourse at Paddington, he vaguely indulged in the futile hope of seeing the humane ticket-inspector. Surely such a wonderful old chap could not possibly have been a mirage? No luck. Instead, he saw what he took to be a far more senior railway-official. The uniform alone was impressive. This was surely the station-master – or possibly the chief of the railway-police?

"Excuse me, please," said Peter. "Could you tell me whether or not steam-trains still occasionally arrive and depart from Paddington?"

"Sorry, sir," said this splendidly-attired individual, "I dunno what goes on no more. I'm retired-like, I just walk around for the sake of old times. I used to be the chocolate-machine replenisher, top grade. No one bothers me and I doesn't bother them."

For Peter, this was another magical oddity in his whole trip to London which added to his happiness. He took his seat in a very nondescript train (one certainly not pulled by a nice old chuff-chuff), and he was thinking of what Anna had said in her flat.

"I believe in your steam-train. It was magical, yes. But magic does happen in real life."

And falling in love, Peter was ecstatically reflecting, was surely the greatest magic of all. He only briefly continued to think about the chocolate-machine replenisher. Peter was never to know it, but the man had been no physical illusion. He was a genuine London eccentric, a former employee of British Rail who had manufactured that splendid uniform himself.

"Chocolate-machine replenisher," was all Peter amusedly murmured. He did just consider, for a second or two, that such a strange figure might be a harbinger of some sort. Perhaps of further trouble from poor old Elsie?

Even this most fearful of fancies was then swept away by the most compelling of reveries. He spent the rest of the journey in recalling every single moment of his encounter with Timothea. Yes, and every single word they exchanged.

He was still in this most beautiful of reveries as his train arrived at Woodley Norton – or, as his maternal forbears would have called it, Widdley Narten.

CHAPTER FIVE

Back to the Cottage

I

Unknown to Peter on that same Sunday, it was a decision by his friend Rafe that was to lead to a rather tricky situation at Peter's cottage.

Rafe had unexpectedly returned from Brussels to his semi-detached house in Hendon (north London). His wife Lizzie was out. Alone in the house, he decided to phone the Golconda Hotel. His breezy charm concealed his worries about Peter.

"Oh, Mrs Collop? Remember me, do you? Peter's friend? Is he there? May I speak to him?"

"Sorry, sir, he's gone back to Oxfordshire."

"Back to his cottage, eh? Right! Thank you very much, Mrs Collop," and Rafe rang off without asking for any further details. He simply assumed that Peter was already back in the cottage.

Hastily, he wrote his wife a quick note after re-packing his bags.

"Lizzie darling, I am just popping up to Peter's cottage. Am very concerned about him. I'll phone you when I get there. Am going by car. Can't stand the thought of going by train. Lots of love."

This meant a stop-and-start journey via the half-completed motorway (which he had campaigned against at its inception).

It also meant a worn-out clutch by the time he got to Woodley Norton. Cursing, he was forced to take a taxi for the rest of the journey to the cottage. In all, this meant he arrived there a full hour before Peter.

"Hello, there," shouted Rafe, through the letter-box. "It's Rafe! Hello!"

Worse was to follow.

Knowing the cottage intimately (from his previous visits), Rafe tried to get into it through the French windows and other points. But Peter's security was too wholesome. Sweating and swearing in the blazing sun ("Oh, bugger! Sod-sod-sod!"), Rafe took himself and his bags into the meadow so appealingly adjacent to the garden. There, in the extreme corner, was the open little summer-house. Finding a folded deck-chair within, he unfolded it and set it up in the part-shadow of the tallish yew trees.

He sat there for half an hour. At least he had refreshment in the shape of a packet of crisps and a flask of whisky. But, although trying to keep an apprehensive eye on the distant bee-hives, he dozed off. He had, after all, come a long way that day – all the way from Brussels. (A top-lawyer kept waiting!)

After nearly another half-hour, Peter was himself delivered, by taxi from the station, to the gate of his cottage. He paid the taxi off (it was not Percy, the village-driver, but a driver from off the rank) and Peter noted the gate had been left open. Peter instantly thought the postman had been and hurriedly unlocked the front door to see if he had a postcard (from the Lake-District, of course). But there was no mail on the mat of any kind whatsoever. He just shrugged and thought: "I couldn't have latched the gate properly."

After a few moments spent in stowing his suitcase and that sort of thing, he suddenly felt happily eager to rehearse.

That's right – rehearse.

He wanted to rehearse what he would say to Timothea when introducing her to the cottage.

"Now here," he said, gesturing like an estate-agent, "we have the lounge. A lot of this furniture, the wooden stuff, I've made myself. This is, of course, a very much re-modelled cottage. It wasn't like this when my mother was a child here. Not by a long chalk," and he opened the French windows wide. "Come into the garden, Timothea my darling sweetie-pie."

Out on the paving stones ("the terrace"), he said: "This, of course, is just the garden-part of my little estate. Mostly wild stuff here, stuff that doesn't need much looking after. That lovely yellow stuff, that's loosestrife, I think."

He walked as if leading Timothea along the path to the wicket-gate in the hedge, stopping just briefly to say: "Oh, and we do have some very nice roses. That's good old fantin-latour, that lot. Lovely fragrance, eh? My friend Rafe put that in some time ago from his garden in Hendon."

Opening the wicket-gate, he magnificently announced: "And this is the meadow. Timothea, my dearest darling Timothea – the Meadow!"

It was at this point in time that Rafe, hitherto unseen in the far corner, began to rise from the deckchair. The expression on his face was one of genuine concern and even horror.

Peter had opened his arms wide and was saying: "Over there, my darling Timothea, you can see – in the distance – the tower of the church where you and I will be married. Look, look Timothea! Look past the bee-hives over there and past the trees. It's the church were my mother's forbears are sleeping – which of course means my forbears too! Ha ha."

Rafe came striding through the long grass and towards Peter like a galleon going at an unnatural speed through the sea. He shouted: "So it's true! You really are bonkers. I didn't like to think so, but now I know it's true. The fact has to be faced. Bonkers."

Peter's response to this interruption was one of increased blissfulness. His welcoming smile could not have been a greater contrast to Rafe's fierce scowl.

"My dear old chap," cried Peter, "where on earth have you popped up from? Come on in and make yourself at home."

"First of all," yelled Rafe, "it's a train that did not run. Then it's a sweetheart who doesn't exist – a sweetheart who is a total hallucination. I find you actually talking to this delusion of yours!"

"Come along, old chap," insisted Peter. "Come indoors. Got any bags with you?"

Indoors, and over a meal and a shared bottle of wine, Peter had a hard time in convincing Rafe that he merely been rehearsing.

"Rehearsing, you say," said Rafe. "You were hallucinating, not rehearsing."

"No, no," said Peter, pleasantly but firmly. "I know it sounds potty, but I was simply trying to work out what to say to her. I'm not used to this sort of thing."

"Frankly, old boy," said Rafe, who was still fairly terse, "I think you need to see a shrink. That bloke in Gower Street might do. I can't remember his name though. He's attached to the University."

Peter was becoming aware that he needed to be careful at this point of friendship. In his life so far, he had learnt that people who are so concerned for the problems of others are often, without knowing it, more concerned about themselves. Their problem can be very spiky and nasty but too well-hidden to be obvious. But a friend can tell, can't he? And he needs to say something, doesn't he?

"Actually," Peter therefore said, "I think it's you who needs to see a shrink."

Rafe looked as if he would explode at the very idea of this suggestion, but the telephone happened to ring – which was over on the sideboard.

"Oh do excuse me," Peter was able to say, and he went to the phone in a rush of excitement.

It was not Timothea, as he had hoped, but it was at least news of her.

"Peter," said Mrs Collop, "I thought I ought to phone and let you know. Your fiancée phoned the hotel today, but it was just after you left to go home. It was one of the girls who answered. She didn't quite know what to say, but I've just found out. The call was made and I thought you ought to be told. Is that all right, Peter?"

"Of course it's all right," cried Peter. "I'm so glad you've phoned. Thank you very much indeed. Goodbye Mrs Collop, bless your heart."

Peter returned to the table and said: "That, as you may have gathered, was news about my hallucination. She phoned the hotel just after I had left. Isn't that amazing? I must have missed her by a whisker!"

"My dear chap," said Rafe, instantly and contritely, "I'm so sorry I wrongly accused you. I'm totally delighted. Mind you, I could cheerfully murder old Ma Collop. She gave me to understand you'd be at home. Hours I had to wait!"

The latter statement was not true, and Peter knew it but merely said: "Let's not quibble over Mrs Collop. Oh, this is such a relief to me!"

Rafe said: "As a matter of fact, dearest Peter old chap, I'm relieved too. I must be honest with you. I had begun to think Timothea was a figment of your imagination. Either that or a ghost."

Peter laughed in all his happiness and said: "Surely you've never believed in that sort of rot?"

"No, not really," said Rafe, and rather red-facedly. "But you surely know how I must be feeling? If that train you were on was not real, then you and Timothea were not real either. Nor me or anyone else. We'd all be phantoms. There wouldn't be any reality to life. It would mean that reality itself doesn't exist. It's the thought of that which scares me stiff. Total horror."

"I do see what you mean, old boy," and, in saying this, Peter realised that he could afford to be decently untruthful about the train. His friend was so sensitively distressed. So Peter said: "As a matter of fact, I could have been mistaken about the train. It could easily not have been a steam-train."

Rafe, although still frowning, was so relieved by this that Peter felt well-justified in having said something he did not believe. Furthermore, this dubious act of friendship led Rafe to say: "Also, my dear friend, you're right about the shrink. I'm the bloke more in need of one. Psychologically, I'm a mess."

"My dear old boy, surely you exaggerate?"

"No, Peter. It's true," and Rafe had put his elbows on the table and sunk his face into this hands. "Nobody really knows how bad I feel. Peter, I have to tell you something," and he looked up haggardly. "I'm absolutely in love with Anna, with Miss Yosenhants, my executive secretary."

After a long pause, Peter said: "Tell you what, old chap. Why don't you smoke one of your very nice cigars?"

"But you don't like people smoking here!"

"Not pipes and cigarettes. But, although I don't smoke cigars myself, I now welcome that particular type of pong. I've discovered," he falsely said, "that cigar-smoke deepens patina."

Having retired to more comfortable chairs, the two friends were soon at ease in the manner of their youth. Canoeing on the upper reaches of the Thames and fruit-picking in the work-camps were still the strongest of memories in the fading evening light of that momentous Sunday. But Peter could see that Rafe was near to exhaustion at the conclusion of just one cigar and the tot of port at his elbow.

"It's an early night for you, old boy," Peter said to Rafe, as if to a child – a child very like the child Snookie had been. But a child with a plump moustache.

II

On the Monday morning, at a mushroom-breakfast (cooked and served by Peter), there was a long silence between the two men.

It was the silence of unbreakable friendship, a silence which had no need for cross-examination of the kind between mere acquaintances. Each friend simply waited for the other to impart further information – if they so chose.

There was, of course, the occasional social phrase or even sentences for enabling life to move on. Peter, for example, said: "I'm going to start work, this morning, on a very nice desk I've been restoring. I'm rather eager to finish it. An engagement present, you see, for Timothea. Would you care to come into the workshop and see what I have to do?"

"Gladly," said Rafe, and he meant it; but his genuine interest was overshadowed by his need for Peter's help. (Rafe was almost hopping from one leg to the other in his increasingly frantic state of mind.)

The workshop, converted from an ancient cow-barn, was alongside a part of the garden just outside the French windows and fronted by Peter's daisy-loaded lawn. ("What is a lawn without daisies," he would say to those who criticised it.) As for the workshop's interior, it was deliciously fragrant with wood-shavings and the toffee-like smells of staining and polishing.

The half-finished Sheraton writing-desk was standing in a space beside Peter's centralised work-bench. Peter put on a dark blue apron before proclaiming his handiwork.

"There it is," he said, grandly gesturing.

"Very nice," said Rafe, sincerely but a shade heavily.

He patiently allowed himself to be shown the desk's major feature (in Peter's eyes) of the beautifully-fitting drawer. It was in a lovely little enclosing cabinet to the back of the table.

"You see?" cried Peter, as he opened and shut this drawer. "Try it yourself! Feel that little puff of air as you close the drawer!"

Rafe felt the little puff of air and agreed that it did indeed signify workmanship of a superb standard. As for the dovetails, who had had ever seen such delicate beauties?

Peter began discoursing as if he were lecturing at the trade-technical in Woodley Norton. He spoke of Sheraton cabinet-making as not really being Sheraton as such but copies of his designs – and often very mixed copies at that. ("This piece," he said, stroking it, "was probably made in 1890 but sold to me as Sheraton. Ridiculous!")

He was not just discoursing, of course, but, to put it bluntly, he was procrastinating. He was mildly fearful, as any friend would be, of being asked to act as a go-between.

The fearful moment came. Rafe, who was genuinely in torment, imploringly said: "Peter, could you possibly do me a very great favour?"

"Of course, old boy," was Peter's instant but rather nervous reply.

"If you could phone the office and tell Anna, Miss Yosenhants I mean, that I'm not very well, I'd very much appreciate it. I did leave Brussels in a bit of a hurry and she might be a little cross about it."

Peter was about to hedge tactfully but was saved by the phone bursting into a ring. (He had an extension in the workshop.) Rafe literally shook all over and sprang for the door.

"It's all right," the ever-hopeful but reassuring Peter cried, "it's probably Timothea."

He was wrong. It was not Timothea. It was Anna, Miss Anna Yosenhants herself – and, as Rafe had predicted, she was very cross indeed.

"I know he's there," she said, in the coldest of voice. "Put him on."

"You want to speak to Rafe, do you?"

"I want to do more than speak to him," was the answer to this. "Put him on."

From around the edge of the door (yes, he was hiding behind it like a guilty small boy), Rafe silently and frenziedly mouthed "No, no!"

Peter was forced to tell a lie on behalf of his friend. He said: "He's not immediately available. I think he may have gone down the Meadow to listen to the bees. He likes the sound, you see. Sort of soothes him."

"Very well," said the frozen-steel voice, "tell him this when he returns from listening to the bees. Tell him that I shall resign, as his secretary, if he's not in the office tomorrow morning at ten o'clock exactly. I shall offer my services to Mr Partridge who is eager to acquire them. Have I made myself clear?"

"Yes, Miss Burgess," said Peter, lightly trying to act as peacemaker. "But may I just say that I – "

Peter was interrupted by the sound of the distant-end phone being plonked decisively down.

Rafe crept back into the workshop from behind the door and Peter said: "Sorry, old chap. I wasn't able to do much for you. She's going to resign, she says, if you're not in the office at ten sharp tomorrow morning."

Rafe was not only gravely disturbed but puzzled. He said: "Who the hell is Miss Burgess?"

"An old head-mistress. Just a teasing reference."

"Oh, Peter," said Rafe, in utter misery, "what am I to do?"

"We'd better ring the garage in Woodley Norton and see when your car will be ready. You'll have to go back by train – this afternoon – if there's any delay. You must be back tomorrow."

"Peter, I mean what am I to do in more general terms? I'm not joking. I really am at the end of my tether."

Peter took off his dark blue apron and hung it up. He said: "I do have an idea in more general terms. Come outside, my dear old friend, and stand with me on the lawn."

"On the lawn? What ever for?"

"I want you to stand, with me, among the daisies. To me, you know, they are the most beautiful of all flowers. Stars in the grass, I call them. Came up this year very early. Amazing!"

"Peter," said Rafe, "I'm asking you to be practical. Why are you rambling on about daisies?"

Peter led the vaguely protesting Rafe to the centre of the daisy-lawn and said: "Rafe, look down at them all. All these daisies."

Rafe looked down at them and said: "So what?"

"What a pretty sight they are! Eh? Agree?"

"Well, yes. They are a pretty enough sight, but very ordinary."

"Rafe, old boy, I now want you to think of the real stars – the stars in the night. Do you remember how bright they used to be? When we were kids during the War? Sprinkled all over the night sky?"

"I remember," said Rafe.

"A breathtakingly beautiful sight, my dear friend. Now what I'm suggesting, old chap, is that you need a hobby. Not," he hastily said, "the same hobby as mine. You'll never learn even how to knock a nail in."

"That's very true," agreed Rafe. "But what hobby have you in mind?"

"The stars, Rafe – the stars! I want you to buy a good telescope and take up astronomy. Study the stars."

"Oh, no," quavered Rafe. "I couldn't possibly do that! All that space! All that infinity! It would scare me to death."

"But Rafe, the stars will protect you from all that inifity. They will be a crystalline barrier as it were, between you and the infinity you're so afraid of. You can even set up a telescope here if you like. Construct a little observatory."

It took only a few seconds for Rafe to emerge from his depression and say: "By God, Peter, you're spot on! That's what I'll do. I'll take it up. I'll take up astronomy. And yes, you're right. These are lovely little flowers," and Rafe seized Peter by the hand and shook it with the biggest smile on his face than Peter had seen for days.

Peter made the phone call. Yes, the car would be ready in four hours time. He said to Rafe: "All we have to do now, old boy, is to get you over to the Woodley Norton repair-garage. Let's get you packed up."

In contrast to the spiritual nature of Peter's suggestion, Rafe instantly became hearty and coarse.

"Bugger the Woodley Norton garage! First things first. I've got to do something for you, my dear old fellow. You and I need to motor over to Stratford. We need to check Timothea's address. See if it's genuine."

It was now Peter's turn to demur and hang back. "Things are all right for me, Rafe. I'm the one on holiday. You are not. You need to get back to London."

"Not until we've checked," said Rafe, "that your Timothea actually exists. We need cast-iron evidence."

"We'll have all the cast-iron evidence we need," Peter tried to insist, "when she comes back to Stratford from the Lake District."

"We need to drive over to Stratford," said Rafe, loudly and firmly. "Get the car out!"

"No, old chap," Peter blushingly said, "we really do need to respect Timothea's wishes. She's having problems with her son and her ex-husband. I can't get in touch before Saturday."

"But you haven't actually checked in person where she lives? Have you?"

"I've looked at the Stratford town-map. I know exactly where she lives."

"But you haven't checked, have you? And what about where she actually works? Have you checked that? One must always check. Facts are essential to our sense of reality."

It was not long before the more strident Rafe had his way. With Peter at the wheel of his old Ford, and Rafe with the open town-map on his lap, the two friends began the investigation of the address provided by Timothea.

They entered Shakespeare's Warwickshire town of Stratford at eleven o'clock. On the way over from Poyton, Rafe could not have been more happily relaxed and buoyant. He kept saying how "marvellous" he felt and how amazingly well-disposed he felt to the entire human race.

"I've had some dealings with shrinks," he enthusiastically told Peter, "and I don't mind saying I reckon you'd make a better job of it!"

"I don't know a lot about that sort of thing," said Peter, and it was true.

"It took you just a few minutes to put me on the right track! How many shrinks could do that? With you, no waffle. No hair-splitting theories. Just good old British common sense! Astronomy! That's the solution for all my troubles. I can't wait to get going. Stars in the grass, eh? Ha!"

Shakespeare's town was full of motor-traffic and tourists on foot, as Peter had tolerantly expected. He had only minor difficulties in finding somewhere to park the car. This was the first thing to affect Rafe's new-found love for the human race. ("Why do all these bloody foreigners want to come to a town like this?")

The second thing was more complex and serious and was related to Timothea's address.

This address turned out to be at a convenient distance from the town-centre. It was a block of flats, but in no way typical of the flat-roofed type the word "block" so often suggests. It was designed to look like a modest mansion and was quietly set back in a less crowded road. Peter was instantly entranced by it. To think that this was where Timothea lived!

Rafe, by contrast, was frowning as he and Peter approached by way of the facing road.

They entered the small courtyard in front of the building. It had tubs of flowers here and there which seemed to increase Rafe's suspicion. Also, it had several marked-out privileged parking-spaces. These positively annoyed Rafe. He said: "Why couldn't we have parked somewhere here? Why have we had to walk all this way?"

"Sorry, old chap," said Peter.

"Not your fault," snapped Rafe, and he began to inspect the door-buttons beside the building's main front door. "These," he added, "are obviously for the upper-floor flats. Ah!"

He had spotted that Timothea's flat was one of several with a front door, on the ground floor, which opened on to the courtyard itself.

"This is it," declared Rafe. "Well? What do we do? See if anyone is at home?"

"If there is," said Peter, in his mild way, "it won't be Timothea. If I undertood her correctly, she is in the Lake District with her sister – and presumably with Timothea's son."

"And when did Timothea say she would be back?"

"In exactly six days it will now be" said Peter, happily and proudly. "Saturday!"

"Well," said Rafe, "let's just see if anyone is at home. Someone minding the flat, perhaps."

Before he could press the bell-button, the door was opened and a young man with binoculars around his neck began yelling hysterically.

Peter recognised him as the young man he had seen on Paddington Station – the pedantic son, the very son Timothea had herself mentioned.

"Go away," he all but screamed. "You're the old man who tried to molest my mother at the station! Don't think I didn't see you. I saw you try to kiss her her. I saw you through my binoculars. Auntie Molly! Come quick! It's that man! I've just seen him walking up the street! There's another one with him! Two dirty old men."

The woman whom Peter also recognised (and who had been referred to by Timothea) joined this hysterical young man from within. She protectively said: "You two men must stop pestering my sister. Go away," and she pulled the young man back inside and shut the door.

Peter was a bit upset at having his illusions about Molly being shattered (he had assumed their relationship would be a happy one), but the effect upon Rafe was far worse. He began banging on the door and even kicking it. Peter literally had to drag him away from it.

"Who the hell," stormed Rafe, "do they think they are? That oik called us dirty old men. My God, Peter, this is too much."

Peter had more than a little difficulty in getting the blaspheming Rafe to the distantly-parked Ford. Rafe was bent upon returning to Timothea's flat and renewing his assault on the door. Peter literally had to hang on his arm more than once.

"It's just a misunderstanding," he kept saying. "Things will simmer down, I'm sure."

Finally, he managed to say something which astounded Rafe so much that he ceased to struggle.

Peter said: "After all, we do have to remember Shakespeare. This was his very own town."

"Shakespeare?" bellowed Rafe. "What the hell has Shakespeare got to do with it? We've both been accused of being two dirty old men."

Peter explained: "I'm only guessing, I admit, but I believe Timothea must have encouraged her sister – along with the difficult son – to make use of her flat for a few days. As I say, this is Shakespeare's town. There's the theatre and all that. It's a cultural treat for the boy so that she, Timothea, can have a bit of peace and quiet in the Lake District."

Rafe said: "A cultural treat for the boy? For a boy who spies on his own mother? Through a pair of binoculars! I'll give that mother-fixated oik a cultural treat when I finally catch up with him," and Rafe did look as if he meant something worse.

This worried Peter. Once back at the old Ford, he made the exit from Stratford as fast as he safely could. And he rather hurriedly prepared a lunch in order to get Rafe over to the Woodley Norton garage as soon as poss. But Rafe was in a doggedly stubborn mood. Even the threat of Miss Anna Yosenhants no longer seemed to intimidate him. He behaved as if he had all the time in the world to finish, sprawlingly, his after-lunch cigar.

"Peter, old sport," he said, "did I hear you say last night that you got a glimpse of those people at Paddington?"

"That's right, yes. They were waiting at the barrier for Timothea."

"And did that oik have his binoculars with him?"

"He was at some distance away and I can't say whether he did or not. But, if he had been using them to spot his mother, then I can only say he couldn't have been using them efficiently."

"You mean he couldn't have seen you trying to kiss his mother?"

Peter blushed. "I don't like to say this, old chap, but I didn't try to kiss her. I did kiss her."

"And she reciprocated?"

"Of course she reciprocated! Rafe, old boy, this isn't a subject for discussion."

"Of course not, old boy," said Rafe. "I'm sorry. I'm not prying. Just getting the facts. And one fact is, I do have to say, that these people could easily verify whether or not you and Timothea arrived on a steam-train."

Peter was now becoming uneasily aware that Rafe was harbouring an obsession about the steam-train. There was a strange glitter in Rafe's eyes. It worried Peter that it could be something unhealthy. Something mentally unhealthy.

Suddenly and sharply, Rafe said: "I think we should phone that flat and get what information we can from those two! You've got the number?"

Peter tried to speak soothingly. "My dear chap, everything will become clearer very soon. But I do have to comply with Timothea's wishes. She asked me not to try getting in touch until she herself is back in Stratford. So let's get you back to London, old chap. Your Miss Yosenhants was very, very angry with you."

"All I want to know," said Rafe, glowering like an open stove, "is whether or not that bloody train of yours was real."

"As I say, old boy, that will all be up for discussion later. For now, we must get you off to Woodley Norton," and Peter tried hard to induce the packing of bags.

"Tell you what," he added, trying to sound cheerfully offhand, "I think you should take a couple of pots with you – as a sort of peace-offering to Anna. Honey, of course. Tell her it's honey from the meadow bees. I think she might like that."

"Peter," said Rafe, becoming distraught, "what the hell are you talking about now?"

"Just two pots of honey, old boy. I did promise to let her have an odd pot or two."

"When? When was this?"

"When we were having lunch on Friday."

"Lunch?" Rafe shouted. "You had lunch with that professional female smoothie? Where?"

"At the Golconda," said Peter in all his innocence. "I invited her there."

Incredulity smote Rafe like falling masonry. He had leapt up out the armchair but slumped back into it.

"God Almighty," he moaned. "I've known her for only three months. But you've only known her for five minutes. Yet it's you she goes to lunch with! At the Golconda of all places, that ghastly emporium of cabbage-water and monkey-nut cutlets. I tell you, Peter, this is all too much. She rejects every lunch-invitation I offer."

Realising that it would be unwise to mention the spaghetti at Anna's flat, Peter tried his diplomatic best to restore Rafe to his normal self.

"Actually, old chap, she was trying to be helpful both to you and to me. She wanted to discuss the matter of those awful phone-calls you've been getting from Elsie."

"She had no right," said Rafe, and not without petulance, "to mention them. I didn't want you to know how really bad that wife of yours had got."

"That was very kind of you, Rafe, but Anna was too worried about it all to keep it to herself. She has, in fact, been intercepting some of the calls."

This was information which surprised Rafe, and he said: "Really? Why did she do that?"

"She thought it best to relieve you of having to cope with Elsie. She may keep you at arm's length, old boy, but she's very loyal."

Rafe began to look pleased again. He stood up to say: "Peter, old lad, I really don't know why you ever married such a foul woman. It's something I don't want to discuss, but I do feel a very real concern."

"That's very decent of you, old chap."

The packing of the bags was resumed with Rafe in a better frame of mind. He accepted the two pots of honey for Anna and a two further pots for Lizzie. Nothing more was said until Peter was prevailingly driving off to Woodley Norton.

He said, after negotiating the bend in the lane: "I only want to mention one point about Elsie. I don't think she's as bad as we might be thinking. I've discovered that she's very probably under the influence of my brother."

Rafe said: "I wouldn't wish to coment on that, old boy."

"Of course not, no," said Peter.

"The only thing I would say, though, is that he's a bit of a slimy sod. I don't like having to say so."

"Of course not, no," said Peter.

Nothing more was uttered until this pair of close friends were nearer to Woodley Norton.

Peter said: "One thing more, old boy. It's about Anna."

Rafe became agitated. "Oh, don't go stirring me up on that subject!"

But Peter, as we know, was capable of reproof. He doggedly said: "Do you remember mentioning to me the matter of love at first sight? In your office ?"

"Of course I remember! So what?"

"People don't talk very much of something very similar. I think it could be called friendship at first sight. It's every bit of a delightful and deep experience. And that's what happened between Anna and myself after you introduced us. We both now know that we're friends for life."

Rafe exclaimed: "By God, I wish I could say that of a woman like that!"

"Actually, Rafe, it could be very much like that for you if, in my opinion, you stop thinking of Anna as a possible sweetheart. After all, you and I are the same age. We're old enough to be her father."

Rafe emitted a very heavy sigh and said: "I do know what you mean, old boy."

"And I think you perhaps need to bear in mind that she obviously has her own private circle for that sort of thing."

"What sort of thing are you talking about?"

"The sort of thing that independent women get up to these days. You surely know what I mean?"

Another heavy sigh from Rafe. "Yes, old boy, I do know. One does hear things. But she's not a tart, I'm sure of that."

"Oh, definitely not a tart. We must never think that of her. It's simply that she's entitled to a private life. She's free to make choices."

"I fully agree, old boy," but Rafe sighed again, and very wistfully. "Yet some older chaps do seem to get lucky. That famous old chap who died a few years ago was actually older than us. He was fifty-four when he got together with a sweetheart of seventeen. They had eight children. Eight!"

"Rafe," said Peter, rather sternly, "who are you talking about?"

"Charlie Chaplin of course!"

"Rafe," said Peter, "you are not Charlie Chaplin. You don't, in any case, have the right sort of moustache."

They had arrived at the quiet forecourt of the repair-garage in Woodley Norton.

Rafe was most contrite in settling his bill while leaving Peter to transfer his luggage. He was even self-critically fingering his plump moustache. After silently shaking hands and getting behind his wheel, he lowered his window to say: "Goodbye, old chappie. Bless your wicked old heart. Thank you for everything."

"Think nothing of it, old boy. Just make sure you get to the office nice and early tomorrow morning. And give my love to Lizzie-Wizzie."

It had been quite an embarrassment for Peter to be so stern with old Rafe. He waved goodbye in some relief. Getting back into his car as soon as Rafe was out of sight, he was soon smiling.

He was giving no further thought to recent events. He was too eager to get back to the cottage – and to restoring the Sheraton-style writing-desk for Timothea. He was hardly able to think of anything else. He didn't even notice, as he pushed open his own front gate, that the Clematis Montana no longer over-hung it quite so much. This was the work of the conscientious Mr Mullins. He had cut it back during Peter's absence in Stratford-upon-Avon. (Mr Mullins, it has to be said, would have liked Peter to have the terribly old wooden gate replaced. But Peter had always pleasantly refused.)

CHAPTER SIX

Well Done

I

During the next four days, Peter became so immersed in the restoration that he was like an absorbed artist in a tropical paradise. He was alone on his own desert island. Only the slightest of breezes rustled the trees, the flowers and the grasses. No one rang the door-bell and no one phoned. This was because almost everyone he knew thought he was away on holiday. He was supremely contented. He had not even remembered that he had cancelled the milk-man. (Yes, there were still milk-men in those days.) Peter was only vaguely puzzled to find that he had no milk to put in his tea. For him the writing-desk had become an embodiment of all his love for Timothea. He simply had no feeling for the passing of time, so much so that he failed to realise that he was still receiving no post-card of any sort he had earlier been longing for.

It was on the Friday that he finally finished "tamping down" the substitute for the mouldering writing-leather. (This was an especially-stiffened piece of dark green canvas which did indeed look far more attractive.)

"That," he said aloud, grinning in satisfaction, "is far better than any piece of a suffering animal – and it will last many years longer!"

He was unable to resist calling upon the help of Mr Mullins, the bee-keeper, who was messing about with some of the empty hives.

"Sorry to trouble you, Mr Mullins, but could you very kindly assist me in moving my latest work of art? I need to get it into the cottage. It's not quite ready, but I want to see it in position."

After being transported by way of the French window, the desk was positioned in the lounge of the cottage but in front of the separate window overlooking the Meadow.

Peter stood back in contemplative rapture to say: "There you are, Mr Mullins! My wife will be able to see your bee-hives when ever she sits down to read or write a letter."

"A very tidy bit of work," said Mr Mullins, "if I may say so. But don't it need a chair?"

Peter quickly chose the best possible chair and Mr Mullins nodded approval before clumping off through the French window. (He was no old yokel, let remind ourselves. He was an up-and-coming young countryman of twenty-two.)

Peter continued to contemplate the desk as if he could see Timothea sitting at it. His calm happiness was sweet and touching to see, but he was brought to himself by the sound of something dropping into the letter-box.

It was a post-card, but not from Timothea and not of the Lake District but London. And it depicted the Changing of the Guard.

It was signed "Anna."

Her inscription simply read: "Well done."

This, he smilingly inferred (and he was right), was a congratulatory reference to having successfully brought Rafe to order.

He looked at his watch. The time: noon. He decided to make himself a spot of something to eat. He had gone without breakfast in his eagerness to finish the desk. All it needed now? A little beeswax.

II

At five minutes past noon that same Friday, Rafe was opening a slim package in London – at his desk in his office overlooking Russell Square. A document-package.

It had been delivered five minutes before by special courier. Betsy (Anna's secretary) had brought it in.

Rafe's fingers trembled as he skimmed through the documents the package had contained. He was obviously shocked and distressed. He was hardly able to press down the lever-key on his intercom.

"Betsy," he managed to say, "please ask Miss Yosenhants to pop in and see me. Immediately."

"Oh, sorry sir," she replied. "It's Friday today. She's gone home."

"As early as this? Couldn't she at least have stopped until one o'clock?"

"She needed," said the reverential Betsy, "to translate the corporation-tax report in peace and quiet."

"Get her on the phone," Rafe quite savagely said.

"What, sir? At her flat?"

"Just get her, Betsy," and Rafe weakly got up after putting the phone down. He went to the window. He looked down at Russell Square.

A "ting!" from the phone. Rafe picked it up, and said: "Is that you Miss Anna Yosenhants?"

"No, sir," said Betsy, striving to be just as professional. "I can obtain no reply, sir."

"Then get my friend Mr Peter Smith on the phone. At once, please. Thank you."

Rafe's hands were shaking so much that it was doubtful that he could have dialled the number himself. Or was it that he was unwilling to? This was a question which even Rafe could not answer.

Peter was easily obtainable. He said: "Hello again, old boy! Everything all right?"

"Er, yes. Everything all right your end?"

"Oh, very much all right! Rafe, I have just finished Timothea's writing-desk. Mr Mullins and I have just placed it in a jolly nice position. Overlooking the Meadow."

"Well done," said Rafe, rather mechanically. "I. er, was just wondering if … "

"If what," asked Peter, joyfully impatient.

"If you don't mind the fact," said Rafe, "that I gave all four pots of the honey to Anna. I wanted to please her. I know you wanted two of the pots to go to Lizzie but I sort of forgot that."

Peter was unaware that Rafe was obviously evading the real reason for making the phone-call. He laughed and said: "No need to feel guilty, old chap. I have lots of honey. Pots galore."

"Peter," said Rafe, trying to be more resolute, "when are you expecting to see Timothea?"

"It will be, I'm sure, some time tomorrow – Saturday. She ought to be back from the Lake District by then."

"Have you tried phoning the flat?"

"Of course I have. But no reply. I think the pedantic son and his auntie have probably left, but I shall see for myself tomorrow. Rafe, is this what you're worrying about? That I'll get more trouble from that quarter?"

Peter had at last sensed that Rafe was worried about something, but Rafe, having now lost every vestige of nerve, seized upon this false explanation.

"Well, dear boy, I have been a bit worried about that completely uncalled-for scene … "

"Not to worry, old chap," cried Peter, and rang off with the happiest of chortles.

Rafe sunk his head in his hands after putting the phone down.

But it "tinged" again and he picked it up wearily. The short talk with Peter had literally exhausted him.

"I have now obtained Miss Yosenhants for you, sir," said Betsy, and Anna came on the line to say: "Well, sir? What is it?"

"Miss Yosenhants," said Rafe, as if he were being strangled, "I desperately need to see you."

"Desperately? Is that really the right word?"

"It's the only word I can think of," said Rafe, and was quite unable to utter another syllable.

Anna said: "I've no intention, sir, of coming back to the office today. If, however, you are as desperate as you say, then you'd better come straight to my flat. I believe you know where it is, sir. Just around the corner, sir."

This cool response galvanised Rafe into putting the phone down and promptly shovelling the documents back into the Courier-envelope.

He was on his way across the Square in seconds, his hands still trembling in clutching the envelope and with his face working darkly.

He was breathless by the time he reached the front door of Anna's flat, having used the punishing stairs rather than the lift.

"For God's sake let me in," he said, as soon as Anna opened the door.

She opened it wider and Rafe shambled over to the sofa and sat down helplessly.

Inclined to be a little satirical, Anna said: "Have you done something terrible? Is that what you're going to tell me?"

"I suppose," Rafe managed to say, "I could be accused of having done something terrible. To employ a private enquiry-agent to spy on one's dearest friend could, perhaps, be described as a terrible thing to do."

"Unspeakable, I would say," said Anna very coldly.

"I only did it," Rafe miserably mumbled, "because I thought he was suffering from some sort of delusion. I wanted to find out if this Timothea of his was a real person. I couldn't really believe she existed."

"Perhaps," said Anna, "the word 'ridiculous' would be a better description of your behaviour."

Rafe jumped up off the sofa and waved the enquiry-papers in Anna's face. She had needled him a little too much. He said: "Ridiculous or not, the fact is that Timothea does not exist."

Anna actually laughed as she backed away, saying: "Now you really are being ridiculous!"

"Perhaps," said Rafe, "I should more accurately say that Timothea no longer exists. She is, in fact, dead. That certainly means she doesn't exist, doesn't it? What say you to that, Miss Yosenhants?"

Miss Yosenhants looked as if her face had been slapped. Horrified, she whispered: "Do you really mean this?"

"Anna," he said, his anger fading, "I'm afraid it's true. She was alive on Sunday, I know, because she rang the Golconda to ask to speak to Peter. But he had left the hotel. That Mrs Collop rang Peter, at the cottage, while I was there, to tell him so."

"But Timothea left no message for Mrs Collop to pass on?"

"Apparently not. But Peter was delirious with happiness just to get the call. It even temporarily convinced me. Timothea was real. She existed."

"Have you rung Peter since you got these horrible reports?"

"Read them for yourself, Anna."

"I don't want to. Did you ring Peter about them?"

"Of course I rang him – not half an hour ago!"

After a shocked pause, Anna said: "And I don't suppose you had the heart to tell him what he obviously didn't know."

"I didn't have the courage, Anna."

"I mean, Rafe, that you didn't have the heart. I know how you must have felt."

This was the first time she had used his name in this way, and, for a moment or two, they stood looking at each other like two frightened children lost in a dark forest. They had to make a real physical effort to sit down on the sofa – in an attempt to think and talk in the way that grown-ups should.

Anna quietly said: "When did she die?"

Rafe looked through the papers, although he did not need to, He said: "She never got to the Lake District. She was taken ill, it seems, in Carlisle. Her relatives put her into a private clinic. She was there for several days before she died the day before yesterday. A major bleed of the brain or something. You must read it for yourself."

Rafe tried to force the papers upon Anna. She ignored them and sprang up to say: "We need to see if Peter knows about this. The relatives you've mentioned must surely have got in touch with him. But it's possible they haven't," and Anna was already dialling Peter's cottage after quickly consulting her meticulous address-book.

He answered within seconds because he was still in the lounge and had been gently bees-waxing the writing-desk.

"Peter, it's Anna. How are you?"

He laughed and said: "I think I can safely say that I'm in my seventh heaven. But how about you, Anna? Everything all right?"

"Er, yes," said Anna. "There is just something I wanted to ask you …"

Anna was just as reluctant as Rafe to speak of what she knew, but her evasions were far more skilful. Forcing her voice to stay steady, she asked: "Peter, do you have any immediate plans?"

"Oh, plenty," Peter cried, and he instantly began rattling them off. "The first question I'll have for Timothea tomorrow will be the question of our honeymoon. I shall be suggesting we go to Southwold – just to see the sea – and then pop straight back to the cottage here! I'm getting it all nice and ready. Also, of course, she may want to continue working. But I'm hoping she might consider giving all that up because I would very like to have a dog. Two dogs, in fact. But I've never been able to have dogs because I'm away so much. I – "

Anna interrupted. "Peter, have her family been in touch with you yet?"

"Not yet, no," said Peter. "Things on that score might be a bit tricky. Timothea does have a rather difficult son."

This was dangerous ground and Anna could not trust herself to go any further. There were tears in her eyes. She quickly said: "I'll have to go now, Peter. Thank you very much for the honey. I've already tried it – on toast for breakfast."

"And thank you," said Peter, on his high wave of gaiety, "for the post-card. Both our grandmothers used to take us to see the Changing of the Guard," and then Peter added something that seemed very strange to Anna.

He said: "I like those two words of yours – well done. I would be very satisfied, I think if that's what could be put on my tombstone. Just those two simple words: well done."

"Peter," said Anna, and she had to swallow hard, "what on earth are you talking about?"

Peter was quick to ask: "I haven't upset you, have I? I'm sorry. It's just that it simply struck me that one should try to lead a life that is worthy of just those two simple words."

"Peter," Anna said, more firmly, "please keep in touch over the next few days."

"Of course," he said.

"Goodbye for now," and she put down the phone.

For a few moments, she remained as if frozen to the receiver she had replaced. Suddenly, she went over to the sofa where Rafe was slackly holding his investigative report. She seized the pages from him, ruffled through them and then threw them back at him in a fit of self-contempt.

"My God," she said. "Did Peter tell you of any other occasions when Timothea tried to contact him?"

"Well, no," said the bitterly confused Rafe. "As I understand it, when I was at the cottage, she only tried to contact him just the once. At that hotel of his. It's one of the reasons why I began to think I should have Timothea investigated. This whole matter has been so very strange."

"More than strange," said Anna, shivering all over. "This is getting harder and harder to think about. I invited him to come here to talk about what was troubling him. That's why he left the hotel – to come and see me before he went off back to Oxfordshire. Had I gone to the Golconda, he would have been able to speak to her for what would have been the last time."

"Surely," said Rafe, feebly trying to be helpful, "you're not going to blame yourself for that?"

"I can't help blaming myself," snapped Anna. "I shouldn't have intruded. Had it not been for me, he could have spoken to her. I gave him spaghetti – and not very well cooked at that."

"Anna," said Rafe, "you cannot expect to be in successful control of everything – including spaghetti."

This was not a tactful thing to say to Anna. She turned upon him with instant fury – well-controlled fury but fury nonetheless.

"This is the wrong time for a quarrel," she said, "but get this straight. I don't seek to control anyone – not even the most gorgeous of men I sometimes choose to test out. All I am ever trying to do, sir, is to sort out my feelings and my life in as careful a way as possible. Even in this day and age, it's what every woman of spirit has to do. Is that clear?"

"Well, yes," said Rafe, who hardly understood a word. "I'm sorry. I apologise."

"And also," she powerfully added, "get this straight. I do not test out my friends. In fact, I rather despise the men I test out. They all turn out to be the same Mr Wrong. Well, sir? How about you? Are we now friends or are we not? Answer me!"

Rafe weakly said: "I do hope we're friends. Of course I do. But what can we do about Peter? How best can we help him?"

Her fury vanished as quickly as it had risen within her. She quietly sat down opposite Rafe and said: "We wait. We do not intrude. We wait until he needs us. We certainly don't continue to put private detectives to work. How much did all that intrusive information cost you?"

Rafe sighed heavily and said: "Too much for me to confess to, I'm afraid. It was their 24-hour provision. Over a dozen operatives were involved. Very proficient. A very, very expensive report."

"Burn it," said Anna, and she stood up to show him the door. "You'd better get back to the office – or to lunch if that's what you want."

"I'll send out for sandwiches," said Rafe, weakly trying to make a little joke. "Unless, of course, I'm to be offered spaghetti here."

"Rafe," said Anna, tossing back her hair, "I wouldn't recommend my spaghetti to anyone. Peter was polite but clearly disgusted. I beg you. Try to stay as calm as you can over the weekend. I'll be in close touch with you and Lizzie."

Rafe lingered unhappily in being ejected. He said: "Will it be all right if I ring Peter from time to time?"

"Of course it will be all right – provided you don't say anything unwisely premature. Initially, simply be prepared to listen."

"But if he doesn't know what's happened, shouldn't we be the first to tell him? We, his friends?"

"Certainly not," she sharply said. "Do you want him to find that you have put private detectives on his trail? Snooping into his private life? And Timothea's?"

Rafe looked so stricken that Anna went on to say: "Stop worrying. If he doesn't know she's dead, he will soon find out. And something he said to me on the phone makes me believe he will take it all in his stride. He's that sort of man. I daresay lots of other people have said what he said. But it convinced me that he's that sort of man. Please go now, Rafe," and her voice trembled as she hurriedly shut the door upon him.

Rafe stood outside the door, staring at it and then talking to it closely and imploringly.

"Anna, I'm worried about the scene I made when I forced

Peter to take me to Timothea's address! I was very uncouth. Timothea's fatal condition must have been known to the people there. Anna!"

No response. Exhausted, Rafe rang for the lift.

III

On the Saturday morning, Peter arose early. He finished all the commonplace chores by nine o'clock. All the laundry was done and dried and every room was spick and span.

Did he try to ring Timothea at Stratford? Of course he did, at half-past nine. He was in no way disquieted on hearing the "number unobtainable" signal. He checked with the Exchange and was told: "This number is no longer in service."

This, too, did not disquiet him let alone enlighten him. Such was the optimistic power of being in love. He simply assumed that Timothea was joyfully severing her connections with Stratford and was eager to move into the cottage. Also, he totally discounted the fact that he had received no further news of her. For Peter, her call to the Golconda had been glorious enough.

His own phone rang at quarter to ten.

He dashed over to the sideboard, fully expecting the caller to be Timothea.

It was Elsie, his former wife.

He was disappointed only for a moment. He gaily said: "Why, Elsie! How nice to hear from you!"

In her dull, flat voice, Elsie said: "Pete, I'm sorry I spoked to you so nasty the other day like. I dunno what come over me."

"Please don't worry about it. I knew you didn't really mean it."

"I has runged you up, Pete, to wish you all the best wishes in the world. That's all I can say about it really. I feels real happy about it. Real happy."

"But Elsie, you must come to the wedding."

"Oh, Peter – you wouldn't like that."

"It would be good for both of us," Peter lightly but firmly said. "You will receive an invitation very, very soon."

After a pause, Elsie said: "All right," and put the phone down. She was obviously as happily ignorant about Timothea as Peter. Elsie's call touched him deeply. It lifted his spirits to an even higher plane of delight. He was soon in the garden in his best tweed suit and, of course, his tweed cap. This was still early summer. It would be July before the garden came into its full fragrance, but, for Peter, the garden was already achingly fragrant and reminded him so much of Timothea's kiss after she and he had got out of the train at Paddington.

Moving amid the fairy-like columbines, the ruby-red violas and the shrub-roses, he began picking a posy of the simplest flowers. The whole garden was so softly and cosily beautiful that it was itself mindful of the human heart. His vision of Timothea was so vivid that he could almost see her when he paused and looked around. She was smilingly coming towards him, delighting in the garden. His whole heart lurched at this vision.

Completing the posy, he murmured: "My heart, your heart, our heart."

By half-past ten, he had got the old Ford out of the garage and was on his way to Stratford.

The stems of the posy were wrapped in a well-dampened cloth and enclosed in a plastic bag. This plastic bag was on the passenger-seat beside him.

The town itself looked happily busy.

He drove directly to the flats where Rafe had made such a scene, and he parked without scruple in one of the available parking-spaces.

Holding the posy in one hand, he used the thumb of his other hand to press the bell-push. An elderly lady opened the door. She was not unfriendly, but she was a total stranger and could only respond formally after Peter asked: "May I speak to Miss Timothea Gudgeon, please? My name is Smith. Peter Smith."

The lady said: "You must be talking about the previous tenant. My husband and I have just moved in. We don't know much about it, but we do know she died. That's how we got the tenancy."

Shock, we are told, is a peculiar reaction. It can affect people in so many different ways that it is not always easy to discern. For Peter, this news was simply unbelievable. He had so strongly associated Timothea with this very door and, indeed, with the whole town of Stratford, that it simply could not even be logical that Timothea had died.

"Where," he asked, "did she die?"

"Not here," the lady said. "That's all we know."

Her husband joined her at the door. He was about the same age as his wife but quicker to sympathise. He said to Peter: "Would you like us to put those little flowers in some water?"

"Yes," said Peter. "That might be a good idea."

The husband took the posy in its plastic bag and added: "Would you like to step in for a moment?"

"Thank you very much." Peter stepped inside the flat. It was very small and as impersonal as any ordinary hotel-room.

The lady noted Peter's impression of the place and said: "This is only a service-flat, Mr Smith. We've taken it for three months. A hotel runs it."

The husband had put the flowers in a small vase and had stood it on the very small sideboard. He said to Peter: "Would you like to sit down for a little while? Have a cup of tea?"

"Thank you, but no," said Peter. "You're both very kind. But I think I ought to leave. I'll never forget how kind you've been. Thank you very much," and he moved to the door, which the husband tactfully made haste to re-open.

Peter drove away from Stratford in a stunned state of careful attention. He had been told the truth. All his instincts had convinced him of that truth, but the shock was contradictory. He was incapable of believing the reality.

The shock affected him in two other ways. First and foremost, he could hear no sound. The old Ford had always been a quiet-running vehicle but, on this occasion, it seemed to be wrapped in sound-absorbing cotton-wool. He could not hear the smallest rattle. It was rather like the time when he and Timothea had been in the train-compartment when it was entering Paddington Station. Both time and sound on that occasion had become temporarily non-existent.

The other form of shock to affect him was his choice of route. For all his attentive care, his route was time-consumingly erratic. He had set off in quite the wrong direction, towards the Vale of Evesham, and then had made his way back through all the towns and villages that were so endearingly familiar. Their very names were a comfort to him: Pebworth, Honeybourne, Chipping Camden, Shipston-on-Stour, Whichford, Great Rollright, Chipping Norton … and, all of this time, he imagined Timothea sitting beside him in joyful silence.

But there was a difference as he neared Poyton and the lane to the cottage. His sense of sound was coming back, principally through the sound of June wedding-bells. Yes, there were couples genuinely being married that Saturday and at many a festive point during his journey.

He barely had any petrol left, but just enough to get the old Ford into his garage. He closed the garage-door and the separate gate to it. His front-garden gate was just a few steps along.

Someone had left it open. The postman?

Yes, it has been the Saturday postman. Opening the front door, Peter found just one letter in the box.

He recognised the writing on the envelope. It was Timothea's. We remember, do we not, how she had written her own address – on that train – on a scrap of paper that he had henceforth treasured? The writing on the envelope was undoubtedly hers.

IV

He took the letter, unopened, to the Sheraton-style writing-desk he had prepared. He sat down at it and glanced through that separate window at the Meadow. All the green and coloured growings were moving gently in a very small breeze. For Mr Mullins, of course, this was the time known as the "June Gap" when the bees in the hives have their own little problems. All very normal. But, for Peter, even the bee-hives looked uncannily normal.

Using the antique paper-knife he had given to the desk, he carefully opened the envelope. He looked calm, but he was hardly breathing.

The writing itself was quite firm at the start of the letter but did become a little shaky towards the end of it, as if the completion had been cut short and hurried for fear of interruption.

He did not read the letter aloud, but we can safely assume that he heard Timothea's voice in his head.

"Dear my Peter, At last I have some time to myself to write and tell you how much I love you. I hope you won't think it too awful of me, but I've been so fussed over and spoilt that I haven't had the heart to tell my ex-husband and his relatives anything about our engagement! The only person I've told is a lovely nurse here who is thrilled to bits by our story. I've had to swear her to secrecy! She is going to post the envelope after writing the address of this place on the back, in the way that foreigners do. So please please write to me! You did promise you would and she will smuggle your letter to me come hell or high water. I'm in absolutely no danger of dying or anything like that, so don't you dare start worrying! It's just an unexpected flare-up of something similar I had years ago in Canada. Inside of me I feel absolutely well and fit and very, very clear in my mind! I am determined to be back in Stratford on Saturday because I'm hoping you will come and whisk me away to anywhere you like, but I'm hoping it will be the cottage you mentioned! I've been imagining what it's like and how happy we shall be at long last and for ever I must go now, From Timothea the luckiest woman in all the world."

Peter finished reading this letter and sat still for a few moments, his face blank. He sighed only a little when, on inspecting the back of the envelope, he found no return-address. The nurse, he concluded, had fulfilled her promise to post the letter but had perhaps sadly decided against supplying the return-address. Also, he spent no time in pondering upon the likelihood that he would hear nothing from this obviously possessive ex-family. He refolded the letter, put it back in its envelope which he then put into the inside-pocket of his tweed jacket.

He would henceforth carry carry it there, in whatever jacket he might be wearing, for the rest of his life. Next to his heart.

But what of the time being?

He made himself a cup of tea and got himself something to eat. As darkness fell, he phoned the usual bed-and-breakfast guest-house he had so often frequented, over the years, in Southwold.

"Oh, Mrs Brightwell! How are you? It's Peter Smith here. May I just book one night for my annual visit to Southwold? You do remember me, don't you?"

"Of course I do, Mr Smith! We were wondering if you would phone. This is your usual date."

Peter was surprised. He said: "Is it? Oh, I suppose it is! I'm in need of a glimpse of the sea. So I'll be driving over tomorrow, arriving at about one. Will a spot of Sunday lunch be possible?"

"Oh, yes Mr Smith!"

"Splendid. I'll be popping back home on the Monday afternoon. I might even have a paddle before I come back."

Mrs Brightwell giggled brightly. "I'm sure that will be lovely for you, Mr Smith."

Her words were so warmly comforting that Peter was reminded, and not for the first time, of both his grandmothers. He therefore said: "I shall be bringing with me not two pots of honey but four pots of honey. An extra token of my esteem and all that. See you tomorrow," and he rang off a shade abruptly, but this did not puzzle Mrs Brightwell. She had long been familiar with the oddities of one of her favourite gentlemen.

He was up at half-past five the following morning, the Sunday. It was to be another developingly light and sunny day. He quickly prepared for the journey to Southwold which meant, of course, packing the old blazer he had worn all those years before. It also meant giving petrol to the old Ford from the spare tin of petrol (enough to get him to the nearest filling-station). Peter had always strived to be methodical. And, of course, faithful to his promises. That is why, before he set off, he sat down at Timothea's writing-desk and began to write a letter. He had promised to write one, had he not? So that is what he did, and in the same optimistic spirit as Timothea's.

He wrote quickly and unhesitatingly. His handwriting was distinctive. (He had always used the Greek E, for example.) He wrote, of course, with a fountain-pen (which he carefully filled beforehand).

Having completed the letter, he read it through, aloud, just the once. His voice was calmly serious. No one, if they had heard him, would have been able to detect any evidence of the cold stone of sadness within him.

"Dear my Timothea. Thank you for your beautiful letter. Beautiful because it is so filled with hope and joy. It was delivered here yesterday, just after I had left to drive over to your flat in Stratford. You were not there. Only then did I realise that we had said goodbye, at Paddington, without either of us knowing it was a real goodbye. While I was driving away from your flat, I felt as if you were sitting beside me. But, this morning, you have gone. You are not here. You are not in the cottage and you are not in the garden or in the Meadow. I am this morning going to drive over to Southwold to see if you might somehow be among the holiday-makers there, perhaps on that lovely stretch of firm sand at low tide. I'll wear my blazer, the one you remember. Perhaps, when I get back here, I will find that you have somehow managed to get back to this my cottage, your cottage, our cottage. I'll be back by tea-time tomorrow. I shall be hoping and expecting to somehow be here with you for the rest of my life. Ever your Peter."

Having finished reading this aloud, Peter did not seem to know what to do next. He took an envelope from the fretworked section (for stationery,) but then put it back. To some of us, perhaps, it seems a silly and fanciful letter, but it was a private letter. And lovers are entitled to be privately silly and fanciful, are they not?

With a shrug and a sigh, he decided quite simply to put the letter in the little well-fitting drawer – the drawer which emitted a puff of air when pushed shut. He then got up and left the desk to do something else which could be thought silly and fanciful. Before finally setting off for Southwold, he picked a tight June rose from near the front door. Peter was not much of a gardener himself (he left all that to Mr Mullins) and did not know what kind of rose it was. It was simply a "very nice" red rose and neatly small enough to put in the lapel buttonhole of his best tweed jacket.

It was to be a long journey across the counties of Northamptonshire, Bedfordshire, Cambridgeshire and finally Suffolk, but he knew the route and the best route. After all, he had been indulging in this silly and fanciful bit of behaviour for years. The only difference was that he had not previously worn a rose.

"That's a bit extraordinary," he said to himself, on arriving in Southwold.

The rose, in his buttonhole, had expanded during the journey. (He had supposed it would have wilted.)

He bestowed the pots of honey upon the good Mrs Brightwell and was able, that same day, to have an after-lunch paddle. He had changed into the old blazer (but with new white trousers, which he rolled up for the paddle). Having transferred the rose to the blazer's buttonhole, he removed it and dropped it into the sea at his feet.

Some holidaymakers around him looked at him suspiciously, so he picked up the sopping-wet rose and put it in the side-pocket of the blazer.

After an early breakfast the next day, Monday, he took the rose back with him to the cottage; but without really knowing he was doing so. (He had left it in the side-pocket of the blazer and had packed the blazer without removing it.)

He unlocked the front door and let himself in.

CHAPTER SEVEN

A Call from the Cottage

In the evening of that same Monday when Peter had returned from Southwold, Rafe was at his home in Hendon (North London). He had agonisingly been obeying Anna. All that day at the office had been, for Rafe, an inner hell of indecision. He ate his evening meal with Lizzie without relish. Anna had been briskly busy all day and had coolly avoided making any reference to Peter. Rafe was thinking: Peter must surely know, by now, of Timothea's death?

The phone rang.

As in almost every suburban type of highly conventional home, the phone was inconveniently situated in the hall at the bottom of the stairs. This hall was always draughty even in summer, but Rafe shivered as if it were winter as he lifted the dreaded receiver.

The call, as he feared, was from Peter, but, to Rafe's surprise, Peter's voice seemed perfectly normal.

"Hello there," he cheerfully said to Rafe. "Is everything all right with you?"

"Er, yes," said Rafe, almost dropping his cigar. "But is everything all right with you my dear old chap?"

"Oh," said Peter, "I've got some simply wonderful news! And of course I am just back from Southwold."

"Oh, really? Southwold, eh? Ah!"

Peter said nothing more for a few moments, so Rafe cautiously said: "And what is this, er, simply wonderful news?"

"I don't want to talk about it over the phone, old chap. It's a bit personal. I've been thinking. Would you and Lizzie-Wizzie like to come here, next week-end, say? I'm still on holiday and I won't be going away. Have you bought your telescope yet? If so, bring it with you old boy!"

"This is very nice of you," Rafe mumbled, and, before he could continue, he was interrupted by Peter exuberantly saying: "That's settled, then! Give my love to Lizzie-Wizzie," and he rang off.

Rafe was so staggered by this call that he had do sit down on the stairs. He was found in this state by his wife who urged him: "For heaven's sake, darling, ring that secretary of yours. Don't try to sort all this out on your own. She's young and fresh."

"And I'm not, I suppose?"

"Not young anyway! Honestly, darling, you're already under enough pressure. If Peter were in his right mind, he wouldn't want to add to it, would he?"

"Of course not, no. I'll ring the young and fresh Miss Frozen-Pants immediately. But bring me a double whisky for God's sake."

If anything, Anna responded to Rafe's phone-call with an even loftier professionalism than we have seen so far. In her well-groomed and decisive way, she cut Rafe short and said: "We must lose no further time. Is it possible to drive to this cottage of Peter's and come back in one day?"

"Well, yes," mumbled Rafe, "If one starts out reasonably promptly after breakfast."

"Then that's what we'll do. You are, of course, familiar with the route to this rustic restreat."

"Yes," Rafe humbly said.

"But you are in no fit state to drive there. I, therefore, shall drive in my own car to Hendon and pick up you and your wife at eight o'clock. Tomorrow morning! Got that?"

"Yes, Anna," said Rafe, even more humbly.

"You shall act as my navigator. And pack on overnight-bag. It's possible things are worse than we fear. Peter must have discovered by now that Timothea has died. For him to talk of having good news after she dies from having had a subarachnoid haemorrhage is very peculiar."

"Should we consult that psychiatrist-chap in Gower Street?"

"Don't be silly, Rafe. No time. We, his friends, have to deal with this as best we can. No strait-jacket is immediately required, I'm sure."

"What about the office?"

"Don't worry about the office. I'll phone up the Senior Partner and, of course, I'll be briefing Betsy. This is a dire personal emergency. Get to bed early. I'll be with you at eight o'clock in the morning," and Anna rang off.

Her plan went well, but not so well when she and her two passengers turned up on Peter's doorstep. She now suffered the same frustration as Rafe when he, too, had turned up without prior notice. Peter was out. Nowhere to be found. Anna felt helplessly angered and tried hard not to show it.

"But it's nearly lunch-time," she frowningly said, consulting her watch. "He ought to be at home! Doesn't he realise how worried we are?"

"Perhaps," suggested Lizzie-Wizzie, "you should have rung him and told him to expect us?"

"So that's it, is it? I'm expected to think of everything!"

Anna was only partly appeased by a tour of the garden and meadow conducted by the very uneasy Rafe. She was still a bit snappy when Peter turned up after an hour with a laden shopping-basket. (He had gone on foot to the village.)

"Oh, how very nice to see you," he said, and he puzzled all three of them by looking so serene. "How about a spot of lunch? I'm thinking of trying out the Golconda Rissole. I was given the secret recipe when I went to London."

His trio of guests were a bit on the silent side as he let them in and served up an extremely good sherry. What does one say to console someone who does not appear to need consoling? Could it be possible that he had not yet learnt that Timothea had died?

Conversation during and just after the round-table meal was awkward until Anna, during coffee, said: "Now look here, Peter. Tell us about the good news you've had. We would like to share your knowledge of it."

All three of them sat forward in their armchairs on hearing Peter say: "Oh, I'm very willing to share my knowledge of it!"

But they were not smiling in anticipation. They were frowning or at least looking worried. The possibility that Peter had somehow "gone mad" was still uppermost in their minds.

Chattily at ease in his favourite armchair, Peter said: "I'm not going to suggest that all three of you sign the Official Secrets Act or anything like that. But I do suggest that we four friends keep this wonderful bit of knowledge to ourselves. It's wonderful but not believable."

Peter's voice trembled slightly on that last sentence. Deliberately, Anna spoke in a matter-of-fact tone. "Just get on with it, Peter."

As she had intended, he adopted her tone. But he did not appear to be willing to enunciate the words "death" or "dead." He seemed to be skirting around that part of the explanation.

"I drove over to Stratford, you see, on Saturday. To Timothea's flat. She wasn't there. I was told the reason for it by the two very nice people who had become the new tenants."

"In other words," said the ever-intelligent Anna, "it's a service-flat. Tenants come and go at short notice. Virtually a hotel-adjunct."

"That's right," said Peter. "Actors and people like that, I suppose. What they told me was a bit of a shock, I do have to say. But, as I drove back here, I was able to imagine Timothea sitting beside me. Do you all understand what I mean?"

"Of course, yes," all three assured Peter, and Rafe added: "A perfectly natural thing to imagine, my dear old chap. We've realised, er, what's happened."

Peter had suddenly become pensive. But not sadly pensive. A smile was lighting up his face. He even gave out a happy little laugh.

"You see," he went on, "that feeling did wear off a bit. I felt very cold inside of me when I unlocked the door and came in. But guess what. I found a letter from Timothea in the letter-box."

And Peter now produced the letter, in its envelope, from his inside pocket.

"It had been delivered," he said, holding it up and waving it, "by our Saturday postman while I was on my way to Stratford."

Anna was the first to recover from this poignant surprise. She said: "We don't expect you to let any of us read her letter." (A chorus of of-course-nots backed up her words.) "But I think it would help us to understand your feelings if you would let us know how she herself felt."

Peter returned the envelope containing Timothea's letter to his inside-pocket. He more quietly and seriously said: "She had every intention of defeating what she saw as a temporary illness. Her main and only problem, as she saw it, was her ex-husband's well-meant efforts at reconciliation."

Anna said: "And was this the only letter you have ever received from Timothea?"

"The only one," said Peter, putting his hand over it (through his covering jacket). And he sighed in adding: "She had to smuggle it out with the aid of a friendly nurse. She seems to have been in some sort of private sanatorium. Before she was taken ill, she did try to phone me at the Golconda Hotel. But I wasn't there, I'm sorry to say. Not to worry, though," and he began smiling again. "I had yet another and bigger surprise!"

His trio of an audience exchanged concealed looks of despairing curiosity and hope – hope, that is, of a genuinely happy ending to

Peter's tragic loss. It hardly seemed likely, yet he sprang up from his chair and began to look brightly excited.

"I do have to admit," he said, "that I did start to feel sort of cold inside and hollowed out as it were. So much so, in fact, that I decided to pop over to Southwold – which is, of course, where I first caught sight of her so many years ago."

"And what was the point of doing that?" asked Anna, still in her matter-of-fact tone.

"I thought it would help me to get more feeling back into me," was his simple reply. "But, before I went off to Southwold, I sat down at this very desk to reply to Timothea's letter."

And he sat down at the desk he had so lovingly restored. He went on to say: "She had asked me to reply, so that's what I did. I wrote a reply in the same spirit as she had written her letter to me. But I felt a bit daft once I had finished writing it. I didn't even know the address of the sanatorium or whatever it was. No address was given. But, even if I had known the address, what point would there have been in sending her my reply?"

"What point indeed," said Anna.

Rather coyly, Peter said: "And so what do you think I did?"

"Just tell us," said Anna.

"I decided," said Peter, smiling at all three of them, "to fold the letter up and just put it in this little drawer," and he extended his fingers to the little drawer's little handle. "After all," he added, "this is her own very personal desk. This little drawer is surely the best possible place to leave such a letter, don't you think?"

"Peter," said Anna, speaking carefully, "I don't think we quite understand what you're telling us."

"What I'm telling you," he said, rather mischievously, "is that I got back from Southwold. I opened this drawer. The letter had gone."

Rafe was the one to say: "Gone? You mean disappeared?"

"Put it that way if you like," said Peter, pulling open the empty drawer, "but I'm putting it differently. Timothea has in some magical way been able to take delivery of my letter."

He displayed the empty drawer before re-inserting it and pushing it back in place.

"Are you saying," said Rafe, looking very disturbed, "that Timothea is actually in this cottage at this very moment?"

"No, Rafe," said Peter. "I know you won't believe me, but she's never in the cottage when I'm in it. She seems to be playing a bit of a game. She's either in the garden or in the meadow when I'm indoors. But, if I go out to find her, she nips back in here – through the open French window, I'm sure. It's why I leave it open," and he gestured at the open French window. This made Rafe even more disturbed. Peter went on: "You can disbelieve me if you like, but I'm hoping that won't affect our friendship. I simply want you to realise that I'm perfectly all right. I don't want any of you to worry about me," and he broke off to say: "Excuse me. I need to do the washing-up. If there's one thing I can't stand, it's people like Snookie Wookie neglecting to do the washing-up," and he went out to the kitchen.

"I'll come and help you," said Lizzie-Wizzie, leaving Anna and Rafe together.

Rafe half-rose from his chair and whispered to Anna frantically: "I do hope Lizzie-Wizzie doesn't say the wrong thing to Peter."

"Sit down," Anna told him, "and don't worry. Your wife will be saying all the right things to Peter. You're the one who will be saying the wrong things if you don't calm down."

"Oh but Anna," said Rafe, subsiding into anguish, "this is all so crazy. He's absolutely off his rocker. What can we do to help the poor old chap?"

"We help him," Anna said firmly and crisply, "by giving him time. Meanwhile, we only need to understand why he's taken refuge, as it were, in delusion. He simply can't accept the reality of the facts facing him. But he will, given time, begin to accept them."

"But Anna, there are certain matters at issue which need a

proper explanation. To begin with, who has taken the letter from the drawer in the desk?"

"Frankly, Rafe, I don't believe anyone took it. I think it highly probable that Peter is deluded on that score as well. It's even possible that he didn't even write such a letter."

"But now imagines that he had written it? Is that what you mean?"

"It's a possibility. But you and I only have a few moments to decide our strategy. It doesn't matter one scrap who took the letter – if, indeed, it was taken from the drawer. Perhaps that chap who looks after the bee-hives took it."

"Mr Mullins?" cried Rafe. "Oh, he would never do a thing like that!"

"Then it might well have been Peter's charwoman or someone of that sort."

"He doesn't have a charwoman. He does all his own washing-up and so on."

Anna almost lost patience with Rafe at this point. She said: "Listen, we three have to get back to London this afternoon. We can do nothing more than give him time. The worst thing we can do is to start behaving like a lawyer and splitting hairs. We must behave as ordinary friends would behave. Agreed?"

"I suppose so," sighed Rafe.

A second later, Peter came back into the room, followed by Lizzie-Wizzie (who gave Anna a womanly complicit glance before sitting down). Peter was still serene, but his friend Rafe was becoming even more agitated – despite the orders of his executive secretary.

He rose from his chair to say: "Listen, old boy. I don't want to pry into the contents of the letter which Timothea wrote. But one thing still worries me. Can you tell me? Does she in any way confirm, in her letter, the type of train you and she were travelling on? Does she, in other words, mention that it was a steam train?"

"No," said Peter, pleasantly but seriously. "She didn't mention the train at all."

He flumped down in his chair and seemed more concerned about the success of the meal he had cooked. He said: "Did you all find the famous Golconda Rissole to be reasonably edible?"

"Oh, yes," they all chorused, lying as generously as they could. Anna even went so far as to say: "I thought it absolutely delicious!"

Having lied on his behalf, his three friends were instantly embarrassed (if not annoyed) to hear Peter say: "I'm so glad. Personally, I thought it absolutely awful. I must have got something wrong. Better luck next time."

Anna stood up to say: "Peter, we all thank you for your hospitality today. We do, however, need to get back to London by this evening."

"Oh, I quite understand," said Peter, also rising. "It's been very nice of you all to pop in and see me. I really am grateful."

"All the same, said Anna, and her voice faltered slightly, "please do keep in touch if anything upsets you. We want to do everything we can to help you."

In their murmurings of assent to these kind words, both Rafe and his wife also became rather faltering. Peter's serenity was so hard to understand. He was, as all three of them saw him, being quite deplorably facetious. His manner had something in it for each of them to fear separately – and for their own private reasons. Rafe, in particular, was rapidly becoming crushingly bewildered.

He tried, while desperately shaking hands with Peter, to say something cheerful to match Peter's mood.

"Goodbye for now, old chap," he said. "It's a pity Timothea prefers to stay outside and not come in. It would have been so nice if she could have rung the door-bell and popped in to tell me about the train. A word from her on the subject would have been most helpful."

As if in clockwork response to Rafe's last idiotic sentence, the front-door bell rang very loudly indeed.

Rafe, Lizzie and Anna all instinctively bunched together as if in protection from the evil unknown. Peter was the only one present not to have been startled. Unhurriedly, he went to the front door and opened it.

"Oh, hello Elsie," he said. "What an unexpected pleasure! Do come in."

As in many of that type of cottage, the front door opened directly into the living-room. It was only partly screened by the elegant shelving which Peter had constructed. As soon as Elsie stepped into clearer view, Rafe was the first to recover. He began listening with hostile interest to the woman he had silently detested for so many years. He was angered that she had frightened him. How absurd to have been frightened by such a mundane woman in a frumpy summer-dress and a frumpy black hat – to say nothing of such a ghastly handbag in the worst possible taste! And that often unintelligible speech!

"Sorry, Pete," were her first gaspingly embarrassed words. "I don't wanna butt in on anyfing. But I needs to see yer. In private-like."

"You are not butting in," said Peter, reassuringly smiling. "You are welcome here. These are my friends. But did you drive here? All the way from London?"

"I duzz, yeah. It won't be in the way, will it? Me car? On the verge just up the lane?"

"Everyone who comes to see me parks there. The vital point, however, is this. Have you had lunch? We've had ours. Is there anything I can get you?"

"Tar very much, Peter, but no. I adda bite in one of them call-in places. I can't stay long, special as you as compnee."

"You can stay," said Peter, firmly, "as long as you like. Everyone here understands this. Rafe and Lizzie you can surely remember. Anna is the only one you haven't met. Elsie, this is Anna."

"Pleased to meetcha," Elsie feebly said.

Anna replied pleasantly and sincerely but a shade

condescendingly; it was always difficult for her to avoid being condescending to people who spoke so terribly badly.

"I'm sure," said Anna, giving a warning glance at Rafe, "that we're all going to be friends."

Instantly, on hearing Anna's voice, Elsie cried: "Oh, miss, you is the one I were speaking to so nasty-like! I really is so sorry! I dunno what come over me. Everyfing is different now, I promise."

"That's right," said Anna, with another warning glance at the glowering Rafe, "everything is different now."

Ignoring the warning glance (which his wife Lizzie had reinforced with a warning glance of her own,) Rafe decided to interpose. It was his duty as a friend, wasn't it? Peter was being so weird. He needed to face reality.

All Rafe's skill as a successful lawyer came to his aid as he sliced into Elsie.

"Elsie," he commandingly said, "why have you come here today?"

She resisted him weakly but stubbornly. "Sorry Mister Rafe sir, but what I has to say is for Peter's private ears and no uvvers."

"Answer my question, Elsie."

"I won't, sir, but I do say to yer as ow sorry I am to have spoke to you even more nasty-like. I aint like that no more. I doesn't do any more phone-calls."

"Elsie, you will answer my question or face some very serious consequences. Why have you come here today?"

Intimidated, she delivered an absolutely startling reply.

"I cummed ear," she said, "to bring back Peter's letter."

"His letter," barked Rafe. "What letter?"

"The letter what e wrote and left in the little drawer of that there desk, I knows all about it, see?"

Both Anna and Lizzie were so stunned by this explanation that they sat down, but Rafe remained on his feet. He knew how to stand up to sensations in court and became even sterner.

"Elsie, are you referring to the letter which Peter addressed to his fiancée? The letter that he later on discovered had gone missing?"

"Yes, Mister Rafe, I've got it in me bag," and Elsie opened her handbag and took out Peter's folded letter. "This is the one. This is the letter, sir."

"How the devil," boomed Rafe, "did that letter come into your possession? Hand it over! Give it to me! At once, Elsie!"

"No, sir," she said, keeping the letter from him at arm's length. "It's Peter's private property. You doesn't av no call on it. Pete's the only one to av any call on it," and she held out the letter to Peter, daringly and breathlessly.

"Thank you, Elsie," was all Peter said, taking it.

He stood still, calmly and silently for a few moments. He held the folded letter close to his chest.

Elsie said to him: "Pete, I were so appy for yer until I redger lovely letter. She's dead, aint she?"

"Yes, Elsie," said Peter, still remaining calm. "Timothea is dead."

Peter's sudden acceptance of the realistic word he had previously been avoiding was a grim form of encouragement for Rafe.

"Now we're getting somewhere," proclaimed Rafe. "Elsie, how did that letter come to be in your handbag?"

He advanced upon her so beefingly that she almost fell over in twisting away. Tears came to her eyes.

"No snivelling," he roared. "We demand the truth."

Anna sprang up at these latter words and said to Rafe: "We are demanding nothing. Sit down, sir, and say no more."

She coaxed the frightened Elsie to an armchair and hovered over her protectively while Rafe angrily muttered to himself. His hesitation was short-lived. His genuinely loyal wife, Lizzie, was quick to support Anna in saying to him: "For heaven's sake, darling, do as you're told. You're saying all the wrong things. Sit down!"

Rafe sat down looking deflated, but he called out to Peter: "I'm only trying to be of help, old chap. These women don't understand."

Peter did not appear to hear him. He was already drifting out through the open French window. It was a perfect June afternoon, with just a slight haze. He sat down in the old wicker-work chair just outside on the flagstones (his "terrace") and henceforth seemed to be dreamily re-reading his letter. Although he had conceded to the blunt word "dead" in applying it to Timothea, he in no way seemed disappointed by what Elsie had begun to say.

"It's all right," Anna whispered to her, "we all want to help Peter. But we're very puzzled. We need to know how that letter got to you in London."

Anna paused to glance cautiously in Peter's direction. He had finished re-reading his letter and seemed content to sit gazing into a visionary distance. He appeared to be untroubled. Although he was still in earshot, Anna was unable to tell whether he was not listening to what was being said, or, in hearing it, was simply indifferent. She was worried by his continuing serenity. It wasn't natural, was it? She fully understood Rafe's bewilderment but was determined to be far more tactful with this simple-minded ex-wife. In the kindliest tones possible, she said to her: "Elsie, you have done nothing wrong. Of that I am convinced."

Elsie's reply was surprisingly spirited. "If you thinks that, miss, then you'd best unconvince yerself double-quick. It aint just that I lost me lilies to Pete's toe-rag of a bruvver. I goes and lets that toe-rag use me motor like it were is own. I has put a stop to all that now, a-course! But that don't mean I aint never done nuffink wrong."

Elsie's now more vigorous voice was a unique mix of old London slang and Peter's army-officer English. Anna warmed to it instantly. Also, having herself "lost her lilies" (and to certain men she had come to despise), her change of feeling towards Elsie sharpened her intuition.

"Elsie," she said, "I think Peter knows exactly what you're going to tell him. He's twigged it. He knows exactly how that letter of his really disappeared from that nice little drawer! He knows, doesn't he?" and Anna raised her voice in Peter's direction on those very words.

Except for a slight smile, Peter did not respond. He had stopped perusing his letter, lightly holding it as he gazed into the summer depths of the garden. He gave every appearance of someone who believes all his guests have departed and left him in peace.

Anna said quietly: "Elsie, when did Snookie Wookie steal Peter's letter from that drawer?"

"Blimey, miss," cried Elsie, deeply impressed, "ow ever didyer know Snookie pinched it?"

"It's a fair assumption," said Anna, and, for her, it was; this example of her talented intuition was why she was a highly-paid secretary. She was quick to add: "Well? When was it? Was it the day before yesterday?"

Faint with awe at this further perception, Elsie shrank back in the armchair and gasped: "Yes, miss. You is right. That's when Snookie dunnit – Sunday."

"He drove up from London in your car, didn't he? Was that with your permission or not?"

"Oh, no, miss! I didn't know e come ear till early this mornin. I went over to is flat, see, to make is brekker. That's when the nasty little toe-rag shows me Pete's letter. This very day! Tuesday!"

"Did Snookie Wookie have a key to this cottage?"

"Yes, miss. Pete give it im for use in case of emergency like. That's as ow e lets isself in."

"And he let himself in, on this occasion, when Peter was away – in Southwold? On Sunday?"

"Yes, miss. That's as what Snookie alwizz duzz when e uses my car to come ear on the scrounge. E knows all the oliday-dates. Snookie is real clever as to what e snitches. Never takes too much. Never takes what might be too quick noticed."

"Then why, Elsie, did he steal Peter's letter? Peter has told us. He immediately noticed the letter had gone as soon as he was back from Southwold."

More spiritedly, Elsie sat up to say: "Yeah, and that was a big mistake on Snookie's part. Im and me was in a bit of contention. I had decided, see, to do no more phone calls. E fort that letter would make me so mad with jealousy that e could get me back on them phone-calls. Believe me, miss, e couldn't ave been more wrong. I gave im a real good thump after I reads Pete's letter. I can't talk all that fine, although I tries, but I can bloody read."

Rafe could no longer restrain himself. He had, after all, endured many months of foul-mouthed phone-calls. He leapt up and strode over to Elsie.

"And what did you do next," he bellowed at her.

"I buggers off from Snookie's flat after taking me car-keys off im. I gets in me own car, which e uses like it belongs to im, and I druvs ear from bloody Ampstidd. Only stops for a bite and petrol."

"And what was your motive, madam? To continue thieving from this cottage?"

It was Lizzie, Rafe's quietly kind wife, who stood up to say: "Oh, darling – do stop beefing."

"This woman," shouted Rafe, "is an accessory to theft."

"It's Snookie who did the thieving," said Lizzie. "Elsie, when were you last inside this cottage?"

"Years and years ago," said Elsie, red-faced and sulkily trying to avoid shedding more tears.

"That's no excuse," the implacable Rafe said. "She has aided and abetted theft by making her car available. I'll ask her again. Elsie, why did you come to this cottage today?"

"I has already said, aint I? To bring back Pete's letter! That's why I was oping to ave a private word like. I were oping I could slip the letter back in the drawer Snookie told me about."

"Hoping, you mean," Rafe triumphantly said, "that Peter

would never know it had been stolen. In other words, madam, you were trying to cover up this latest theft."

In support of Lizzie, Anna said to Rafe: "For all our sakes, sir, do as Lizzie says and stop beefing. Peter's never going to prosecute. Sit down, sir."

Rafe sat down but muttered: "She can't deny that she came here to put that letter back in the drawer. An attempted cover-up. That's collusion."

"Elsie," said Lizzie, "would you very kindly explain, for the sake of Rafe's peace of mind, why you didn't want Peter to know his letter had been taken from the drawer."

Elsie answered a shade petulantly. "I don't know what you think about it all, but I think Pete as enough on is plate. I didn't want im to know ow stinking rotten is bruvver really is. E loves that dirty toe-rag of a bruvver. Always will."

"Thank you, Elsie," said Lizzie. "That's the very answer I was expecting," and to Anna, Lizzie said: "Elsie is a very gallant lady, wouldn't you say?"

"I would indeed," was Anna's serious reply.

"All right," snapped the vanquished Rafe. "What about *my* plate? I've got enough on that as well. A big part of it is that I still don't trust this woman. She's caused Peter a lot of trouble for many years."

It was Anna who said, after exchanging another complicit glance with Lizzie: "Elsie, you have mentioned that you were hoping for a private talk with Peter. In addition to returning the letter, the need for the talk was obviously another reason for coming here. Would you very kindly tell us what you intended to tell Peter?"

"I were intending to tell im – and I still will – that I has decided to sell me dad's house in Hackney. My house, I mean. I'm goin to buy a flat in that nice new block over Dalston way. I won't be no more trouble to Peter. Also, I am getting another solicitor-bloke."

"And that's an answer," said Anna, "of a kind I too was expecting," and she turned to Rafe to say: "Satisfied, sir?"

Rafe grunted. Other things were still disturbing him about Peter, as they were the two ladies; but at least the matter of Elsie's past behaviour had been reasonably settled out of court.

Anna gave Peter another of her many concerned glances, as did Lizzie. From his wicker-chair outside the French window, he appeared not to have heard one word of what been said. He was as still as a rock, although not in any way stony-faced or rigid. The only change in his appearance was that his eyes were now shut. His silence and his lack of response had become, for all of them, a baffling predicament. What could they do to help him?

Anna sighed and turned her concern towards Elsie.

"Elsie," she said, producing a visiting-card from her handbag, "here's my card. Do please get in touch with me if you have any problems with your decision. Moving house can be jolly stressful – to say nothing of changing solicitors at the same time."

"That's very kind of yer, miss," said Elsie, putting the card into her own handbag – the bag that so appalled Rafe.

"Elsie, please don't call me Miss. My name is Anna. I am not your headmistress, nor mine neither."

"Thank you, Anna," said Elsie.

"And call me Lizzie," said Lizzie.

"Thank you, Lizzie," said Elsie and tremblingly added: "You are two very nice ladies."

"Might I ask you, Elsie," said Lizzie, "a rather big question? When did you actually make the decision to sell your house and move?"

"Oh," said Elsie, faintly smiling for the first time, "it were on the bile for quite some time. On the boil, I mean," she corrected herself. "But it didn't come on real strong, as a feeling, until after I finished reading frew Pete's letter."

Rafe, who was still bristling, chose to jump up and say: "Are you in the habit of reading other people's private letters?"

"No, Mister Rafe," said Elsie, ceasing to smile. "Not normally. But Snookie gives me the letter afore I knowed it were a letter. Wodger make of that is all e said. So I has to read it, didn't I?"

"Of course you did," said Lizzie. "Sit down, Rafe. Stop being so nasty. Elsie, you are saying it was Peter's letter that made your mind up? How did it do that?"

Smiling again, Elsie replied happily but a shade vaguely. "Oh, it were because it were such a lovely letter! It got me to understand ole Pete real deep-like. For the first time, see? It changed me all over. Blossomed me out as you might say."

Rafe had not sat down. His frown was dark and his whole face had tightened. He had moved over to the French window. He had stood looking at the unresponsive Peter outside.

Turning back into the room, Rafe confronted his wife Lizzie.

"What on earth is wrong with you two women? Why are you wasting time in gossiping with this foul-mouthed ex-wife? Can't you yet understand," he said, in the fiercest of whispers, "that he's on the brink of total mental collapse?"

Lizzie did her best to console Rafe. She got him to sit down on the cottage-sofa beside her. "Please, my darling, do try to stay calm. We're trying to work out the best way we can all help Peter."

"Then why aren't you making any suggestions? It's time you did so!"

Anna was quick to join Lizzie in dealing with Rafe. She bent over him as if he were a fractious child in his pram. Coolly but strongly, she said: "Sir, please be first in telling us what you suggest."

In his same fierce whisper, Rafe said: "Peter needs to be able to attend the woman's funeral. Do either of you have the common decency to understand why?"

"Yes, sir," said Anna, "your wife and I both hope we do."

The fierce whisper became savage. "I should never have listened to you. I should never have destroyed those details about the poor dead woman. But I still remember them! I know the names and addresses! We need to get in touch with the relatives on Peter's behalf – before it's too late. You're my secretary. Get on with it. Get it done."

Anna drew back a little. Lizzie, sitting beside Rafe as she was, intervened. Hugging Rafe's frigid arm as comfortingly as she could, she said: "Darling, I agreed with Anna about the details. I still do. They are none of our business. It's for the relatives to get in touch with Peter if they think it seemly to do so."

"Seemly?" Rafe almost shouted. "Is it seemly for a man to be deprived of even sending flowers?"

"Rafe," said Lizzie, a shade more firmly, "you are the one who created a scene at Stratford which, as you've admitted, upset the boy and his aunt."

"That's got nothing to do with it!"

"Perhaps not," said Lizzie. "But it's likely that that nurse who posted Timothea's letter has told the bereaved relatives about Peter. We're not the only ones, I'm sure, to be confused about the best thing to do. What ever the situation may be, it's for those relatives to get in touch with Peter."

"If they think it seemly," Anna complicitly added.

Rafe made the feeblest of objections. "But the relatives don't know Peter's name and address!"

"If the nurse has told them about the letter she was asked to post, then they will know," said Lizzie.

"Yes, but what if the nurse has said nothing?"

"Rafe," said Lizzie, more sharply. "Stop it! Stop behaving like this. You'll make yourself ill."

Rafe subsided heavily. He angrily muttered: "We can't leave Peter like this. We need to think of something to give him comfort. Since you two females won't accept my suggestion, then perhaps," and this was suggested sarcastically, "you'd better consult the foul-mouthed Elsie. She was, after all, his wife. She must have something wise to say."

"A good idea," said Anna, severely and seriously, and she turned to address the woman Rafe still despised.

But Elsie was not in the room. She had stepped outside (on to the so-called terrace) and was looking down at Peter. He never stirred. His eyes remained shut. She almost touched his shoulder, but timidly refrained. Coming back into the living-room, she said: "Pete's a real nice bloke, but seems to be gorn a bit funny-like. I reckon sunnick oughta be done, but I doesn't know what. Praps you two nice ladies oughta avver go."

For some reason best known to himself, these words galvanised Rafe. He tried to struggle up from the sofa to go to Peter, but Lizzie strenuously held him back. She implored Anna: "Do see if you can do anything for Peter! This idiot will have a heart attack if we don't keep him calm."

Like all good secretaries, Anna was quick to take the initiative. Her remedy for Peter's funny-like state was immediate and efficient. Stepping outside through the French window, she said to him: "The desk, Peter – Timothea's writing-desk."

He opened his eyes at once and stood up. Although still looking remote, he said: "What about it?"

"Glue," she loudly said.

"Glue?" He repeated the word as if puzzled to the very depths of his soul.

"You have glue in your workshop, don't you?"

"Well, yes. Not animal-based, of course. But I do use glue. One has to."

Anna stepped back into the living-room. Peter followed her as if towed by a short length of rope. She turned to stand and face him.

"Peter," she said, after gently touching the desk surface, "Rafe has told Lizzie and me of how lovingly you restored this desk. He could talk of almost nothing else as we came here today."

"Oh, really?"

"I'm sure Rafe would agree with me in saying that this entire desk commemorates your love for Timothea."

"I'm sure he would. Because it's true."

"That being so, Peter, I suggest that you think about the letter you wrote. The letter you wrote to Timothea."

"Letter?" He had suddenly become vague again.

"The letter," she quietly explained, "which you are still holding in your hand."

He looked down at his hand and said: "Oh, yes … this is the letter you mean. Which she never received."

He began to unfold it, but she said: "No, don't unfold it. Leave it folded up. You see, Peter, it would be a lovely thing to do if you were to put that letter back in the drawer."

"Back in the drawer?"

"Yes, Peter. Back in the drawer. And then, Peter, you must lock the drawer. It has a keyhole, I see. So it will lock, won't it?"

"Yes, there is a key to it. But I didn't lock it when I went off to Southwold. I suppose I should have done. No one, such as Snookie Wookie, could then have taken it. He wouldn't have broken the lock to open the drawer. He would know *that* would arouse suspicion."

"I'm sure you're right, Peter. But that's not the point I'm making. You need to put the letter back in the drawer, lock the drawer and then dispose of the key. Dispose of it at Southwold."

"What? Chuck it in the water?"

"Well, yes. Why not? Not immediately, of course. You could do it when you next pop over to Southwold – as I'm sure you will."

"But I'm puzzled, Anna. You mentioned glue. What has glue got to do with it?"

"I'm thinking of this super-glue stuff that's been invented. You need to squirt it into the key-hole. No one, then, will ever be able to open the drawer even if they find a suitable key."

Affable as he was as a man, Peter was still stubbornly puzzled. "Anna, I can't quite see the point in what you're suggesting."

"The drawer, Peter, will be sealed up for years and years. Possibly for centuries."

"Sealed up? This beautifully-made little drawer?" Peter had now become politely scandalised. "Open and shut it for yourself. Feel the little puff of air on your hand as you push it shut."

Anna opened and shut the drawer and said: "Yes, I agree. It's a beautifully-made little drawer. But that's part of the whole point. To seal up this drawer – with your letter inside it – will be a lasting and beautiful memorial to the woman you love."

"I do see what you mean, Anna. Nevertheless …"

Anna interrupted him by appealing to Lizzie. "Lizzie! What do *you* think?"

Lizzie jumped up from the sofa, her eyes shining with enthusiasm. "Oh, I think it a lovely idea!" and she kissed Peter on the cheek. "Do it, Peter! Think of it. Long after we're all dead and gone, this desk may well need restoration again. It might get woodworm or something of that sort. It would have to be fully and carefully dismantled. Your letter, Peter, will then be found. It will touch the hearts of the people destined to find it. Especially if you put Timothea's letter in as well."

Peter stiffened at these latter words. He said: "That's absolutely out of the question. I don't want anyone else to read her letter. I shall carry it with me for the rest of my life in what ever jacket I am wearing. In my inside-pocket. Next to my heart."

"Of course," said Anna, and Lizzie echoed her and kissed him again.

Anna kissed him too; and there was no further resistance from him over the original idea.

He said: "I do thank you, Anna. I shall never use this desk myself, but it will always be a comfort to me to see it in the room. I have something else which I think I would also like to put in the drawer. Excuse me a moment."

Leaving the folded-up letter on the desk, he went upstairs to the wardrobe in his bedroom. The blue blazer was hanging there. He took the rose from the pocket where he had left it; and he was surprised to see that it was in recognisable condition, despite having been dropped in salt-water. Carrying it gently on the palm of his hand, he re-entered the living-room.

His own four friends (four, that is, if we include Elsie) were standing and waiting.

He said to them: "It's the little rose I took with me when I went to Southwold. On Sunday. I did intend to drop it in the sea, which I did; but I felt a bit awkward, I don't know why. I scooped it up and brought it back with me. In my blazer pocket."

In his calm, methodical way, he laid the crumpled rose beside the letter on the desk. He opened the drawer. He unfolded the letter and laid it flat inside the drawer. He then picked up the rose and laid it on top of the unfolded letter.

He then gently closed the drawer.

He turned to Anna and smiled and said: "It's done."

"No, Peter," she said. "You need to lock it. Where's the key?"

"The key?" He had gone a bit vague. "Oh, yes – the key. It's inside the drawer," and he opened the drawer again, "Ah! There it is!"

He took out the key, which still had the auctioneer's label attached to it, and examined it briefly. He then locked the drawer and stood back. He had put the key into his trouser pocket.

Anna said: "And what about the glue?"

"The glue?" Peter had again gone a little vague. "Oh, yes – the glue. I have an unopened tube of some really good stuff in the workshop. Excuse me again. Won't be a moment," and he went out to his garden workshop by way of the French window.

As soon as Peter was out of earshot, Rafe turned on Elsie with renewed venom. He stingingly whispered: "Now that Peter's slowly getting back to normal, don't you go thinking he will re-marry you."

"Rafe," Lizzie frantically whispered, "how dare you say such a thing! Apologise at once."

An immediate apology was not necessary. Elsie was looking a bit out of her depth (in not knowing everything that had been discussed), but she was no longer frightened of Rafe. She was serious but good-natured. She said to him: "Don't you worry, mate. A second daft mistake won't ever blot out a first one."

"I'm sorry," muttered Rafe, and he sat down on the sofa beside Lizzie and in petulant exhaustion.

Elsie added: "If you was to read Pete's lovely letter, Mister Rafe, you would know what I mean."

Lizzie instantly cried: "Oh, that's just what I've been thinking! Rafe, you need to read Peter's letter."

"I wouldn't dream of doing such a thing," he snapped. "Leave me alone."

"But look what it's done for Elsie! As she has said herself, it has changed her life to see that letter. It will help you pull yourself together."

Anna was quick to agree. "After all, both his brother and his former wife have read the letter. Why shouldn't you, as his best friend, read the same letter? It will help you to understand him a lot better. It's what you need."

"I don't want to read it," snarled Rafe. "I refuse to read it. What I need is to get back to London – and with no further delay."

He got up from the sofa as Peter re-entered the living-room (by way of the French window). He was carrying a small, unopened carton containing the tube of glue. He ripped it open and held up the tube for all to see.

"This is the stuff I mentioned," he said. "It will do the job perfectly," but he saw the look on Rafe's face. He added: "What's the matter? Is something wrong?"

"All Anna and I are suggesting," said Lizzie, "is that Rafe needs to read the letter you wrote. We think it will do him good."

Peter was instantly embarrassed. He even blushed slightly. He said: "Oh, but I don't like the idea of too many people seeing it, – especially not a fellow-chappie like Rafe. I'm sure he understands and wouldn't dream of reading something so personal."

"Absolutely right," said Rafe. "I am in no way like his brother or, for that matter, his ex-wife. A good reason for gluing up the lock, I would say, is to prevent people like them from prying into his private life."

Anna merely had to raise her eyebrows at those last three words. Rafe, still full of guilt about the report he had commissioned, could only sit down on the sofa beside his wife.

"Peter," said Anna, calmly and strongly, "give me the key."

"Key?" Peter had gone all vague again.

"The key to the drawer, Peter, which is in your left-hand trouser-pocket. Hand it over."

"Don't let her have the key," Rafe almost shrieked. "Sorry, old boy, but I have to leave. For London."

Rafe had to struggle to get up off the sofa, but his protest did not prevail. Peter produced the key. He handed it to Anna. He was in something of a trance again. Both he and Rafe were now completely under Anna's command. This was a sight which impressed the open-mouthed Elsie no end.

Anna's next act was to turn towards Rafe and say: "Take it, sir, and unlock that drawer. Read the letter and then put it back."

"I refuse," he tried to insist. "You do it if you want to, but I refuse."

"It's not my place to read your friend's love-letter," she rapped out.

"Nor mine," cried Lizzie supportively. "So do as you're told, Rafe. You'll be helping both yourself as well as Peter. We shall stand well away from you!"

Rafe took the key. He unlocked the desk's beautifully well-made little drawer. Leaving the key in the lock, he pulled the drawer open.

"My God," he cried.

Both the letter and the withered rose had disappeared. There could be no doubting the fact.

"Both gone," he croakingly said.

Anna and Lizzie shared their own sense of amazement after thoroughly inspecting the interior of the drawer. Neither of them could find anything to say in the next few moments.

As for Peter, he simply stood there and smiled. The sight of the empty drawer in no way amazed him.

It was Rafe who said, quaveringly: "What on earth does this mean?"

And it was Elsie, in all her honourable simplicity who said: "It can only mean one thing. It's proof."

"Proof of what?" snapped Rafe.

"Love Eternal," said Elsie.

Both Anna and Lizzie gazed at Elsie in thrilled respect. Anna whispered huskily: "She's right …"

"Rubbish," yelled Rafe, recovering his strength of voice. "She's the one who's taken the letter! And that old rose! She's got them in her handbag. Open that handbag, damn you. Empty it out."

"Mister Rafe," said Elsie, placidly unoffended, "the only person oo could a-took them fings can only be Pete's lady. I doesn't know as ow she did it, but she somehow dunnit and that is that."

Peter had emerged from his semi-trance. He tried to placate his friend by saying: "My dear old boy, I'm sure Elsie is right. Snookie just happened to pinch the letter before Timothea was able to get to it. But now she's got it."

"Rubbish," Rafe desperately repeated .

"Without anyone being able to notice, she perhaps nipped in through the French window – after I'd gone out to the workshop. She took the letter and the rose and nipped out again."

"But the drawer was locked," shouted Rafe.

"That would make no difference," said Peter. "But there's no point in discussing what might or might not have happened. The fact remains. Timothea has now received the letter I promised to write. As Elsie has just said, that's that. Accept it, my dear old chap."

"I cannot," said Rafe, literally shaking all over. With his eyes like saucers, he collapsed on the cottage-sofa. He weakly repeated: "This couldn't have happened. It just couldn't."

Both Anna and Lizzie were in such a state of smiling ecstasy that neither of them immediately appreciated Rafe's deep distress. According to Anna's wrist-watch (which she checked with rapture,) the time on that glorious afternoon was just after four o'clock. For both her and Lizzie, this was a magical time of wonder which they would cherish for the rest of their lives. For Rafe, this period of time was like the witching hour when everything normal and ordinary becomes hideous and frightening.

"Get me back to London," he was feebly saying. "I can't stand this place," and he made several attempts to rise from the sofa to make a dash from the cottage. Each attempt failed, leaving him weaker each time he collapsed.

Although still in something of trance, Peter was the first to make an effort (clumsily, we have to say) to console Rafe. He said: "Don't worry, old chap. Nothing you've done, such as that bit of bother in Stratford, can be the reason for my not having heard from Timothea's family."

"That's not the point, old boy," Rafe managed to gasp.

Peter dreamily went on: "People think of all sorts of strange things when they're upset. The family probably think the shock of meeting me again, on that train, caused Timothea to have some sort of delayed seizure. I'm sure they're wrong, but you're in no way to blame for anything."

Rafe managed to half-rise from the sofa to appeal to Anna. "Anna, get me back to London!"

Anna at once took charge of the situation, snapping into her role as a super-efficient secretary. But not in the way Rafe felt entitled to expect. She laid a hand on his heaving shoulder and lightly but firmly pushed him back on the sofa.

Standing and gazing down upon him, she said: "Sir, pull yourself together," spoken coldly and calmly.

"Get me back to London," he again weakly said. "I can't stand it here. Peter believes in ghosts. He thinks Timothea's ghost took that letter from the desk. It's nonsense. It can only be nonsense. I refuse to believe in ghosts," and he looked around wildly, as if dreading to see Timothea somewhere in the room.

"Sir," said Anna, "your friend Peter is probably quite mistaken."

Rafe was startled by these words, but they did tone him down a little. He plaintively asked: "You're on my side in all this? That Peter is wrong?"

Again Anna spoke coldly and calmly. "On your side, sir, as much as I am on Peter's side. I am not saying he is wrong. I am suggesting that he is mistaken. There is a difference."

Rafe began to bristle with anger. "Don't try splitting hairs with me, Miss Yosenhants. Just say what you mean or shut up."

"In my opinion," said Anna even more strongly, "there is no ghost in this cottage. Not, that is, in the traditional form which seems to frighten you. The ghost, if you want to call it that, is the desk itself. Timothea's desk. The desk which Peter has so lovingly restored."

Rafe's eyes swivelled towards the desk. He stared for a few moments before saying: "What utter balderdash" and slumping back on the sofa.

Anna pressed home her argument with the clever intention, we have to say, of reinvigorating her still very unhappy boss.

"The idea that Timothea, in the form of a traditional ghost, came in from the garden and took the letter from the drawer is, of course, a charming thought. It's even possible, I daresay. But I think it's a lot more metaphysical than that."

"Metaphysical?" Rafe sat up and yelled the word.

"The letter was never extracted from the drawer in any normal human way. Not in my opinion. I believe," said Anna, sounding seriously scientific, "that it was metaphysically absorbed. To us, that simply means that it disappeared. Together with the rose."

Rafe sprang up to bellow: "And how was it, Miss Yosenhants, that Peter's nasty little brother was able to steal the letter?"

"Presumably," said Anna, aloofly, "because Timothea's spirit needed time to find its way to its destination. And to transmute, metaphysically, into the desk. The brother simply happened to get there first."

"As I said myself," Peter put in. "But I'm perfectly willing to believe that it's all been a bit metaphysical. Whatever that means," he added, and began to chortle.

It was a chortle that soon became a happy laugh, with both Anna and Lizzie joining in. Even Elsie was toothily smiling, although still unsure of herself.

Rafe glowered at them all as if they were a gang of miscreants. He barked at Anna: "Get me back to London immediately. I shall never be able to come here again," and he strode out of the cottage (by way of the front door).

The miscreants all followed him down the path and through the gate (and under the overhanging Clematis Montana). Their laughter had diminished to an affable chortle but they were unrepentant.

Anna had parked her motor-car just up the lane and on the grassy verge bordering a grove of magnificently tall trees. A slight breeze, rather like a chortle, was rustling the new leaves.

Rafe was leaning against the wing of Anna's car, his arms grimly folded. Lizzie mischievously said to him: "Rafe, we can't go until you've said goodbye to Elsie. It ill becomes you to be so rude."

Capitulation had never come easily to Rafe, but, within his brusque limits, he did his best to be better-mannered. Elsie was at a little distance away, having modestly waddled over to her own car (a shining and glossy model which Peter had helped to pay for). She was feeling about in her dreadful handbag for her keys. Rafe strode over to her, scowling. He said: "Elsie! Do you share my wife's opinion? And my secretary's opinion?"

Elsie was still toothily smiling. She said: "I dunno, mate. It will allus be a mistry what ever wye we looks at it. Best we say nuffink to nobody. Keep it a secret-like. We shall all be carted orff to the nut-ouse if we so much as breeve a word."

Rafe did not return her smile, but his scowl had vanished. He thrust out his hand and said: "Shake on it, Elsie! You're absolutely right. We must say nothing. Now come over and say goodbye to these other wretched women."

He turned and thoughtfully walked back to Anna's car. Anna was standing beside it, with Lizzie. Both were grinning gleefully. Anna whispered to Lizzie: "See what I mean? He's now a lot more amenable. Most men are nearly always taken in by a bit of gobble-de-gook. You only need to make it seem scientific."

Peter was standing nearby and he overheard these words. He merely smiled and opened the rear passenger door for Lizzie. She ducked inside after calling out to Rafe: "Come along, darling. Look slippy."

Rafe ducked into the back of the car beside Lizzie after waiting for Anna to get behind her steering-wheel. Doors were then shut, but it just so happened that Lizzie wound down her window to speak to Elsie. She had obediently followed in Rafe's wake and was still smiling toothily.

Lizzie said: "Goodbye for now, Elsie! You really must come over to Hendon and see us. It's been years. I'd like you to see what we've done to the place. Rafe, too, would love you to come over. Wouldn't you, darling?" and Lizzie unsparingly dug him in the ribs with her elbow.

He responded sulkily and growlingly. "I suppose so."

To the surprise of everyone, Elsie lumberingly darted closer to the car-window. Almost sticking her head through the opening, still smiling toothily, she replied to Rafe in an extraordinarily different tone of voice. It was exactly like the tone of certain members of the Mayfair upper class.

"My deah fella, thank you so much. It's fraffly good of yah. And of this young gel of yarze. I shall be dee-laited."

There was a second or two of silence before everyone, including Rafe, burst into laughter. It was laughter more joyful than ever before. Rafe himself was actually shedding tears of mirth.

Suddenly, he jumped out of the car. Leaving the door wide open, he began hugging Elsie as if she were a favourite but long-lost auntie.

"Oh, Elsie," he cried, "how marvellous you are! Why aren't you on the stage? How is it we never realised?"

"I dunno," said Elsie, in her normal tone of voice. "I dunno what come over me."

Within the car, Anna recovered sufficiently to twist round in her seat and say to Lizzie: "A good demonstration, don't you think?"

"Of what," panted Lizzie, still in the throes of mirth herself.

"A demonstration of the absurdity of two social extremes of speech. One is just as bad as the other. Quite a political little lesson."

"I'm sorry, Anna," said Lizzie, dabbing her eyes, "I can't be intellectual about all this. All I can do is to be happy – so wonderfully happy. I don't think I've been as happy as this in all my life."

Outside the car, Rafe was saying to Elsie: "Now don't leave it too long. We'll stay in touch," and he jumped back into the car and pulled the door shut. He yelled at Anna: "Back to London! Get on with it!"

Anna drove off expertly and in far more control of herself than Rafe and Lizzie, but there was no mistaking the beautiful spirit of reconciliation possessing them all.

And that included Peter as he, standing beside Elsie, waved goodbye. He said to Elsie: "Would you, perhaps, like a cup of tea before you set off?"

"Blimey, no," she said, and she was already on her way back to her own car. "I can't ang about."

Peter helped her into her car in his vague and gentle way. His love for her (from another part of the heart, as defined by Anna) was now more fond than at any time in their marriage. He was so overwhelmingly grateful for that one pearl of wisdom she had uttered earlier on. It had been a gift beyond price, a gift not only for himself but for Anna, Rafe and Lizzie. He was therefore hoping that she would utter something even more profound on the subject of Love Eternal.

She pulled her door shut with a terse "clunk!" and sat for a moment in stolid silence. She was no longer toothily smiling.

Suddenly, she lowered her window. She said: "Tell me this, Pete. What was they all laughing about?"

He was astonished and disappointed by this question. He said: "But Elsie, you surely know why?"

She was expressing annoyance with him in saying: "If I knowed, I wouldn't be asking. Why was they laughing?"

"Elsie, you were laughing yourself!"

"No, Peter. I were not. I were only smiling-like. You can't elp smiling-like when everyone around is laughing fit to bust. So what was so funny?"

"Nothing was funny, Elsie. They were laughing because you'd been so wonderful. If it hadn't been for you, I and my friends might have split up for ever. Look, do come in and have a cup of tea. Why are you rushing off?"

"It's because I'm going orff on me olidays ter-morrer. First thing. Gotta git meself ready-like. I'm goin wiv Flossie and Trisha. Member erm, do yer? Me two mates from school?"

"I do indeed," said Peter. "Where are you going?"

"Marjorca," she said, pronouncing the name as "Marge-jorkah" with her worst glottal stop. "Aint been there afore. But they duzz fish and chips there just like you gets in London."

Peter could not resist making a little joke in saying: "And eel-pie with garlic? And possibly tripe and onions?"

"That would be nice," said Elsie, in all innocent seriousness.

"Same old Elsie," Peter chortled. "But do remember you're always welcome here. Goodbye. Drive carefully. Have a really good time."

"Wait a minute," she cried. "What are you going to do about your brother?"

"I shall speak to him very severely when I next go to London."

"Huh," she said, with down-to-earth scepticism. "What about the key to yer cottage? You should never ave give ittim. Never!"

"I shall take it away from him," said Peter, "until I'm satisfied that his behaviour has improved."

"Yeah? Well, Pete, I has already got it off im for yer," and she produced the key from her handbag. She passed it to Peter through the open window and added: "Don't you ever lettim ave it back. I aint never bossed you about. But this time I am. It beats me why you ever lettim ave it at all."

"I only gave it to him in case he was evicted from his flat and needed somewhere to lay his head. If I happened to be away, I didn't like to think of the poor little chap being unable to get in – perhaps on a cold night in the middle of winter."

"Aw, for Gawd's sake," said Elsie.

There was only a hint of well-informed impatience in her voice. She was too fond of Peter to make it a stronger hint. He, too, was too fond of her to be as sharp as he might otherwise have been at any hint of well-meant criticism of his brotherly love.

He merely said: "Have you any further advice?"

Said with more vigour: "Yes I has! It's about that desk-thing you done up. Looks real good."

"Thank you, Elsie."

"Tell you what, though. Them two nice ladies seem to think your Timothea is sort of inside of it. I dunno what that means. But I duzz say this. If she can receive your lovely letter, then that might mean that you, mate, can receive a reply to it."

Peter had gone back into his slight trance. He said: "I don't think I quite understand you."

"All you needs to do, mate, is to look inside that empty drawer from time to time. You might one day find a reply. That would be a great comfort to yer, wouldn't it? Well? Wouldn't it?"

Peter's answer to Elsie was as faraway as a half-forgotten dream of heaven. "You're being very kind to me. Thank you for what you're saying."

"What I is also saying," she said, with even greater vigour, "is that you must keep this to yerself. Even if you duzz get a reply, don't ever say one word about it – not to anyone, and that includes me!"

"But Elsie, why ever not?"

"Well, mate, I fer one couldn't cope with the knowing of it. But your best mate, I can tell you, is a nice bloke oo would go right mad. E were always nice to me – well, to begin with. And I wouldn't want im going real mad."

She switched on her engine "And Pete, there's just one more fing. Keep that little drawer locked. Only unlock it when you looks inside to see if you've got a reply. Never forget to re-lock it."

In his faraway state, Peter obtusely said: "Why?"

"Because," she said, and in more obvious exasperation, "you doesn't need to ave some spiteful bugger forging a letter to make a fool of yer!"

Having bluntly said that, Elsie drove away up the lane as expertly as Anna.

There now came one of those detached moments in time which Peter and Anna had discussed at her flat in London. Birds had soon begun hopping about on the surface of the lane once it was deserted. But, suddenly, everything stood still. The birds stood still. All the leaves on the trees stood still.

Peter instantly found himself to be standing still, both in body and in mind. The entire moment had only lasted for a second or so, perhaps a lot less; but it left Peter feeling at one with everything around him. He found himself to be a more integrated human being than ever before.

The birds resumed hopping about and one of them swooped up to perch on the old sign-post at the corner. This was a signpost which had escaped war-time uprooting. One arm was simply lettered "Stratford" (with no mileage given); the other arm was lettered "Woodley Norton" (again with no mileage). Peter gazed briefly at this signpost (which he had known all his life) as if he had never seen it.

He smiled. It was a sad smile, but a smile. He positively strode to his white-wooden gate. He opened it and went through it under the Clematis Montana. Every leaf and flower (even the Clematis Montana) was alert with the presence of Timothea.

"Has she already sent me a reply," he was wondering, and wondering so hopefully that a thrill of expectation was wafting over his whole body.

He re-entered the cottage by way of the open French window. For a few seconds, he could only stand on the threshold and gaze into the room where he had positioned the desk. To him, Timothea was no longer capriciously alternating between the garden and the cottage-interior. For him, she was now more assertively in that room.

But even more assertively in the desk …

Peter approached the desk slowly and in a very mixed state of mind. He took hold of the little handle. He shut his eyes. He gently pulled open the drawer.

He opened his eyes. The drawer was still empty.

His disappointment was so intense that he almost lost his physical balance. Taking refuge in good humour, he pushed the drawer shut and loudly said: "Elsie, my girl, your kind suggestion has not borne fruit. No reply as yet. But I can still enjoy that little puff of air!"

Noticing the tube of super-glue in its carton which he had left on the desk, he facetiously cried: "Back to the workshop with that!"

He snatched up the super-glue in its carton and bounded off through the French window. Back to his garden workshop, he felt magnificently reassured. This was the workshop where he had spent so many happy years, to say nothing of the last few happy days he had spent in restoring Timothea's desk.

Tossing aside the super-glue, he was surprised to find himself saying: "Elsie, my dear girl, you've got things a little bit wrong. I shall never receive a reply from Timothea. That's because no further proof of Love Eternal is needed. That one miracle was enough. I am expected to know that."

He was still sad, but it was a happier and clearer form of sadness. It was even clear enough for him to appreciate Elsie's edict about the desk-drawer. ("Never forget to re-lock it.") Peter's love for his brother was still as constant as always, but he now more clearly realised that Snookie's malice was incurable.

"On that matter, dear Elsie," Peter almost yelled, "you are absolutely right! The little skunk might take it into his head to forge a reply from Timothea."

Peter also suddenly realised something more. He had forgotten to lock the drawer. Delving into his trouser-pocket, he withdrew the key and bounded back to the living-room.

He rapidly opened and shut the drawer several times (just to enjoy feeling that little puff of air on the back of his hand). He then locked the drawer decisively and (as far as he was concerned) for ever.

"This key," he bellowed, copying Rafe's loudest tones, "will stay with me for the rest of my life! D'you hear that, Snookie, you little blighter?"

He removed the auctioneer's label and attached the key to his normal bunch of keys and began to chortle in his old manner.

What more needs to be said about Peter and his cottage?

Was it ever likely that he might one day re-open the drawer? On, say, his ninetieth birthday? Just to check that he had been right about the drawer?

We shall never know.

All we need to know, perhaps, is what he knew for certain himself. Timothea's love for him was not only surviving by being embodied in a Sheraton-style writing-desk.

It was also surviving by being enshrined in the love between himself and his four closest friends.

Rafe, Lizzie and Anna.

And Elsie.

She and Peter had been wrong to marry but now, as friends, were perfect. All of these five friends were now sharing this perfection in the same way. As Anna had said, it was love from another part of the heart.

But it was still love.

What happier form of consolation can there ever be at a time of total loss?

TWO OTHER NOVELS BY D.V HAINES

Enjoyable Motoring (2016)

This novel is a guide to freedom from accident on public roads.

An ardent but tedious motor-accident researcher has persuaded an old-style motorist to lecture to a bunch of modern-day drivers. Essentially, his weird lectures emphasise the difference between motor-sport and motoring. He tries to show how a proper knowledge of this difference will reduce congestion and accidents on public roads.

Will he succeed? Or will his incorrigible audience prefer to go on killing and injuring themselves? Or hanker after a society where electronic control of "driverless" vehicles takes away the freedom of the open road? Although "only a novel", fiction in this form offers many a truth.

The Gentleman Shopkeeper (2017)

In this novel, a different type of gentleman tells his politically-incorrect story in his own blunderingly British way. Reviewers have summed him up succinctly.

Nancy Kline (Goodreads reviewer):
I highly recommend "The Gentleman Shopkeeper" for both its clever intrigue, original and intricate plot, and well-developed characters.

And, whether intentioned or not, it produces quite a depth of psychological insight into human nature.

Brandi Welch (freelance reviewer):
At first, I wasn't sure where this was going and the main character didn't seem to know either. But what a fun read! The quirky characters, the twists in the plot, and the eccentric language all joined together for a really fun time.

Douglas Osler (reviewer):
This will keep you laughing but it is certainly not lightweight. It is a murder story in reverse. Instead of whodunit, the reader knows that from the start and the mystery is what happens next. It is very well written and the main character is typical of buffoons we all probably know.

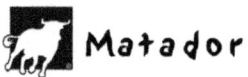 Matador

For exclusive discounts on Matador titles,
sign up to our occasional newsletter at
troubador.co.uk/bookshop